MW01631497

PROTECTING AMY (SPECIAL FORCES: OPERATION ALPHA)

DESIREE HOLT

Thanks for taking the time for this.
Enjoy the Read!
Desiree Holt
XOXO

Editor: Kate Richards
Cover Design: Croco Designs
Beta Reader: Margie Hager

Dear Readers,

Welcome to the Special Forces: Operation Alpha Fan-Fiction world!

If you are new to this amazing world, in a nutshell the author wrote a story using one or more of my characters in it. Sometimes that character has a major role in the story, and other times they are only mentioned briefly. This is perfectly legal and allowable because they are going through Aces Press to publish the story.

This book is entirely the work of the author who wrote it. While I might have assisted with brainstorming and other ideas about which of my characters to use, I didn't have any part in the process or writing or editing the story.

I'm proud and excited that so many authors loved my characters enough that they wanted to write them into their own story. Thank you for supporting them, and me!

READ ON!

Xoxo

Susan Stoker

To Kate Richards and Margie Hager, my wonderful team who make all things possible.

To former SEAL Jack Carr, who inspires my SEAL stories

Thank you for your service.

And to Amy Hrutkay, who is a person I so admire, and who makes life so easy for the authors in the Special Forces World.

And my daughter Amy Nease, a shining light in my life.

CHAPTER 1

It was the screams that woke her. She had fallen asleep early, tired from a long day of errands, and, for a moment she thought she was having a nightmare. Then she heard the scream again, loud and piercing, and her mother's voice shouting. Pleading.

"No. Please, no. I beg you. Please. What are you doing there? Why… God." The scream sliced through the air.

She threw back the covers and ran from her room, racing down the stairs toward the family room, the source of the screams, when she heard them again. This time there were no words, just a screech of mingled pain and terror. She stopped at the sight that presented itself to her. Harrison, her stepfather, lay on the floor facedown, his body at an unnatural angle, the back of his shirt soaked with blood. More of it lay in widening pools around him. Next to him, her mother was curled in a ball, arms over her face in a protective gesture. Blood still welled from a slash on her arm and flowed from two huge wounds to her back. And she wasn't moving, either.

Without looking around, she dropped beside her mother, heart pounding as she pressed two fingers to her throat, feeling a very faint pulse. Tears running down her cheeks, she shifted to check on Harrison. Same results. Who had done this? Why?

"Get away from them." A guttural voice snapped the words.

Pulse accelerating, she turned slowly to see Matthew, her stepbrother, standing behind her, holding a bloody butcher knife. His T-shirt and jeans were covered in blood splatters, hair disheveled, a smear of blood on one cheek. She hadn't seen him in weeks. What was he doing here? Chills raced down her spine, and she found it hard to breathe.

She swallowed hard and forced herself to speak.

"M-Matthew? What happened here? We have to get help for them."

"Leave them, bitch. It's all your fault anyway. You and your smarmy mother and my asshole father. Now, move," he shouted.

But fear froze her in her position.

"I said move. Now, bitch."

He stepped closer to her, and, when she couldn't seem to make herself get up, he raised the knife and slashed her shoulder and her back. Then he stabbed her twice in the side, the pain so sharp and breath-stealing, for a moment she thought she was dead. She collapsed forward, hoping she could stay alive long enough for him to leave.

"What's going on here? Daddy? Why is everyone screaming?"

Oh no! Oh, god, no.

She managed to slide a glance sideways and saw her little brother, Brian, in his pajamas, staring, his face white, stark fear in his eyes.

"Matthew? Matty, w-why do you have that knife?" His eyes were wide with fear. "Why did you hurt them? Why…"

"Fuck," Matthew shouted, the word thick with anger. "You should have stayed in bed, you fucking little brat."

She tried to get up, to get to Brian and protect him, but before she could, she heard more screams. She saw Matthew grab Brian by the neck with one of his thick hands and plunge the butcher knife three times into the small body. When he didn't fall down at once, he kicked him.

She saw the little body crumple to the floor and, with an effort, swallowed down the fear and pain, forcing herself to remain still. Hoping he believed she was dead. The pain was so sharp she could hardly draw a breath. Then she heard the knife clatter to the floor, followed by running footsteps. She raised her head just enough to see what was happening and saw him race for the kitchen and out the back door. She prayed the police could get here in time to save at least one of them.

With slow, painful movements, she inched her way over to reach the cell phone on the coffee table, and...

Amy Ressler woke with a start, sweating and shaking, throat parched and dry and tight with fear. She sat up in bed, clicked on the nightstand light. Her bedroom looked the same as it had when she'd gone to sleep. Nothing disturbed. Nothing different.

Then the images slammed into her, and she realized it was the dream again, the nightmare. As vividly as if they were all here in her room, she saw the bodies on the family room floor, including hers. Felt the burning pain of the stab wounds. Heard the insane sound of Matthew's voice. Would it never go away? Realizing she was shaking, she wrapped her arms around herself. Blinked to clear the scene from her brain.

God. Ten years, and the details were just as vivid in her mind, the fear still as intense and suffocating. At last, when her breathing had evened out, she tossed back the covers and climbed unsteadily out of bed. In the bathroom, she filled a glass of water and looked at herself in the mirror while she drank it. The face that looked back at her was pale and drawn, with dark circles under her eyes. She hadn't looked this bad since, well, since *it* happened.

It.

What a small, innocuous word to describe the worst moment of her life. One minute she was happy and enjoying life, excited about her college graduation and her interview for a dream job. The next she was living a nightmare and changing every aspect of her life just to be able to stay alive. Even after all these years the nightmares still came with regularity and still frightened her to death. Ten years!

Was this what the rest of her life would be like? Would it never stop?

Why on earth when her mother married Harrison Baker had she not put her foot down where Matthew was concerned. Gotten him some psychological help. Everyone knew he had an unnatural vicious streak, that he thrived on cruelty. That there was something wrong with him. Her mother had tried to tell Harrison over and over again that laying down the law wasn't going to fix whatever it was, but he refused to listen.

Now they were all dead, and Matthew was in prison, supposedly for the rest of his life. But Amy would only relax once the man was dead. Something she prayed for on a regular basis.

With tremendous effort, she forced herself to focus on something else. Anything else. The new video game she was designing. The research she was doing for it, the one she titled *SEALs of Glory*. She decided she was in love with all SEALs, the icons of Special Forces. Creating and designing each character and plotting the missions gave her a real edge of excitement. And blocked out the terror that was still her constant companion after all these years. She had planned to use her degree in computer science to write programs for businesses, but this was a lot more fun. Discovering she had the talent and interest for designing these games was the only thing that helped her retain her sanity.

The days after the killings were still a blur. She still gave thanks every day for Harrison's attorney, Dan Rendell, who had worked with the police to relocate her, help her purchase a home and get settled. At least as much as she'd ever be. He was her only lifeline to the world and still handled so many things for her.

When she'd fled Texas, she'd had no idea where to hide or what to do with her life from that day forward. It had taken all her strength to get to Florida and move into the house Harrison had purchased for her in the name of a shell company. Located in South Tampa, the comforting Spanish architecture and mature landscaping of the single-story home gave her a sense of protection. She'd managed to move in, but she hadn't been able to set foot outside since then, not even to the little guest cottage in the back.

Guest cottage? She didn't plan on having any visitors.

"You never know," Dan Rendell told her. "Life can change."

But not for her.

Dan had contracted with an agency named Security

Solutions to provide agents when she needed them, such as when strangers like the landscapers came to work on her yard. She didn't trust Matthew not to reach out beyond prison, if he found a way to do that, and try to slip someone in.

"He's locked up tighter than a drum," Dan assured her. "And if anything changes, they'll notify me at once. But he truly thinks you're dead. The Marshals and I are doing a good job."

But both he and the Marshals who kept in touch with her off and on urged her to rent the cottage out to someone who could provide security on a round-the-clock basis. Have a stranger living here? On her property? Discovering what a nutjob she was? She didn't think so. As long as she never left the house, she'd be safe.

In a new city, living under a new name—new everything—she should be safe. She no longer jumped every time her cell rang, remembering only Dan Rendell and her shrink had that phone number, and his office monitored anyone coming onto the premises, like landscapers and housekeepers. And none of them knew her real identity except for Dan. After ten years, she'd thought life could finally go on for her.

The monster was locked away. Even after all these years, she checked the special site obsessively, needing the assurance he was still in prison. Only the scars that were a constant reminder kept her tied to that night, them and one other thing. Okay, one *very big* thing. A huge thing.

She couldn't make herself leave the house.

She knew it was crazy. Actually, truth be told, people thought *she* was crazy. This year, finally, she had decided to try stepping out onto the patio to have a cup of coffee. But every time she set a foot outside the door, she broke out in a cold sweat, and nausea gripped her. Sometimes it took her half an hour to get back to semi-normal. She had her groceries delivered and hired people for everything else. A housekeeper, a gardener, a repairman, all thoroughly vetted by the police. She'd learned there wasn't a thing you couldn't do either by phone or Internet.

And she had no face-to-face personal relationships, friendship or otherwise. Nothing where her scars would be called into question, despite the fact they'd faded a lot. To her, they were still as visible as when they were fresh, daily reminders of that nightmare. And, of course, there was the terrified state of mind she still had to work hard to control. Even after ten years, all her socializing was done online with people she'd never met.

After all, she couldn't contact people who thought she was dead. Nothing that would give away her location. Which was stupid because *he* was still in prison. She'd found a place online where you could verify the information, and she did so every week without fail. For ten years. Why didn't they just execute him, she wondered. Wasn't killing four people enough of a reason? No matter how much the attorney, who checked on her regularly with a secure phone, tried to tell her it was time to take her life back, the fear was still so overwhelming.

She glanced at the clock. Three a.m. Maybe she'd log onto the chat room she was comfortable in. A few years ago, she'd discovered it while surfing the Internet, looking for someone who might answer a coding question that was giving her fits. She'd fallen into the gaming industry while trying to figure out a way to use her computer skills without leaving the house. Answering an online ad had given her that first break and led her to what was now a very lucrative business for her.

She knew experts were out there, and it wasn't as if she'd have to tell anyone who she really was. Even her chat room name, KitCat for her kitty—one of the few living, breathing things she allowed in the house with her—didn't track back to her. Then, one night, she dropped in an avatar and joined the conversation.

The first two times she entered the room, she'd just observed. She found the people there fascinating and interesting and, at least on the surface, nonthreatening. They came and went, and sometimes months would go by before she dropped in again. On purpose. She didn't want a constant presence that could in any way lead back to her. Just in case. And mostly, she just posted questions.

Which was how, a few months ago, she'd met Tex. Married and over-the-top in love with his wife, he frequently had insomnia and logged onto the Internet to relax at odd hours. She'd taken a chance when she was having a thorny problem with one string of code for the game she was working on. If he was a computer genius, as it seemed he was, maybe he could help her. Depending on what kind of genius he was, of course. When she'd posted her coding question, he'd invited her into a private chat room so he could give her information, but she'd laughed at his message.

Tex: Cute name, KitCat, but I gotta tell you right off, I'm married to the most wonderful woman in the world, and she gets everything I've got to give.

She'd been taken aback for a moment before answering.

KitCat: No prob. I'm not in it for that. A relationship is the last thing on my mind.

Tex: Ever?

KitCat: No, and don't ask Please But Please. But I reached out because I thought you could help me with a programming problem.

Tex: Yeah? You a programmer?

KitCat: I design video games.

Tex: No kidding? Killer.

That first night, she posed her problem to him, and he'd given her what turned out to be a simple answer. The next night, she'd hopped online to thank him, and they began chatting, mostly about their work.

When she first got into the video game design business, she'd discovered a whole room filled with techno fanatics who could answer any question about anything cyber. Especially coding and designing. Over the years she'd made cyber "acquaintances," Tex being the latest.

She was pleased with the fact he was full-out in love with his wife, Melody, who he loved beyond life itself. At least someone had a happy ending. He also told her he was a former SEAL who worked with members of his team, but that other SEALs he knew dropped by from time to time. Some of them were looking for clues on the next step in their lives. That's what had given her the idea for the *SEALs of Honor* game, which she now had a contract for.

They had been chatting regularly since that first time, mostly about computer codes but also about life in general. He seemed to have an innate ability to put people at ease.

She should try and go back to sleep, except she was pretty sure that was impossible, so she might as well distract herself. She looked at the clock again. Three thirty. Patience, her sweet and wonderful cat, followed her down the hallway to her office and jumped onto her lap the moment she sat down.

She woke up her non-work computer and signed in. The first thing she did, as usual, was call up the site where she searched for Matthew's prison status. It was amazing, she thought, how much information was out there if you only knew how to look for it. She breathed a sigh of relief when his name came up as still incarcerated.

She closed out the site, clicked on the link for her favorite chat room, and boom! There she was. And so was Tex. He was exchanging info with someone named Harry about accelerated processors. Tex was a computer genius who helped other people who needed his skills. She'd learned he kept track of his friends so they'd be safe. Which made him an all-around nice guy. And he was the one who seemed to "get" her the most. He somehow sensed her trauma and never pushed, following her lead when it came to anything personal.

No matter what Tex said, there'd never be a right guy for her. For one thing, he'd want her to leave her house and that was never happening. Maybe tonight she'd ask him for more information about the SEALs that wasn't classified and use it to start planning the follow-up games. One thing she'd learned with *Call of Duty*: if gamers loved a particular game, they wanted the next level and the next.

His wife is lucky. I don't think I'll ever have anyone like that.

She began typing.

*KitCat: Hey, Tex. See you're up late, too. Didn't Melody wear you out? *grin**

Tex: She did her best but you know me.

She did. As much as you could know anyone in this kind of environment.

Tex: What are you doing up so late? Bad dreams again?

She had made a slip one night when she logged on at a crazy hour and, without thinking, said she'd been having nightmares from a dangerous experience. She could not imagine spilling all of that to a total stranger. Whenever he asked, she avoided the issue, and he never pushed. She could be anonymous here, and she wanted to keep it that way. They'd again been discussing a string of code she was having trouble with.

KitCat: Bad dreams about a code that won't work. And needing more information about SEALs.

Tex: Okay. Let's hear about it. The coding, first.

For the next half hour, he patiently answered her questions and made suggestions. She opened a document so she could take notes and, by the time they were finished, she was buzzing with excitement.

KitCat: Thank you so much, Tex. I'm excited to get to work on this. I'm going to sign off so I can have at it.

Tex: Now? It's almost four in the morning?

KitCat: So what? You're up."

Tex: But I'm going to shut down and crawl into bed with my beautiful, exciting, sexy, wonderful wife."

For a moment, hot jealousy crawled through her veins. Then she put a hard lid on it. She'd never have that kind of relationship because she'd never be able to trust a man to get that close. Ever. He'd done that, the monster who had killed her family and destroyed her life.

No more pity party, Amy, she told herself. Things could be worse.

Patience, as if seeing her turmoil, pressed against her and purred loudly. What would she do without her?

KitCat: Enjoy. You are so lucky.

Tex: I know. Hey, maybe the right guy will come along for you.

Amy tensed, even though he couldn't see her. There's never going to be a right guy for her. For one thing, he'd want her to leave her house and that was never happening.

KitCat: We'll see.

But she knew the truth of the situation. She was about to say good night when a new message popped up.

Tex: Hey, KitCat? You want to know everything about SEALs? I've got a buddy spending some time with us who's recently out of the SEALs and trying to put his life together. He was a team leader and could give you even more information than I can. Is it okay with you if he joins us online next time? He's asleep right now or I'd go get him.

A stranger? Talk to someone she didn't know? A chill slithered down her back. But wait! He couldn't see her or find her, right? Besides, he was a SEAL, the best of the best, and Tex was vouching for him. Tex, who had proven to be a friend all these weeks and created trust even across the Internet.

Amy, she reminded herself, all strangers aren't like *him*. And besides, *he's* locked up tight in prison.

KitCat: Sure. That would be okay, I guess. Is he into this kind of stuff? Chatting like this, I mean?

There was a long pause that made Amy both uneasy and curious. Was there something dangerous about this man?

Tex: I'm not sure what he's into right now. He's dealing with a bunch of shit, so I asked him to hang with us for a while. He's dealing with an injury from a mission that fell apart and can't figure out the rest of his life. He'd be great in security work, despite his bum leg. I've been trying to hook him up with a friend of mine in Florida, but he doesn't think he can handle the job.

KitCat: A SEAL who can't handle something? That's not what I hear.

Tex: Yeah. I'm trying to convince him.

KitCat: I can relate. I've been there myself.

Tex: I kinda figured, even though you don't say anything. So maybe you and he could chat?

Could she? Talk to a stranger. Well, she was talking to Tex, right? He'd been a stranger in the beginning. The very thought, however, made her mouth go dry and her heartbeat accelerate just a little.

KitCat: I wouldn't know what to say to him.

Tex: How about hello? Nice to meet you. That usually works. Then you can ask him your questions.

Amy swallowed a laugh. Tex probably thought she was the stupidest person in the world. She wasn't.

She was, in fact, very smart, and, until *it* happened, strong and fearless. Why couldn't she be that person again?

Tex: You still there, KitCat?

KitCat: What? Oh yes. Sorry.

She took a deep breath and let it out slowly. She could chat with this SEAL online. Right? He'd be at a safe distance. He might not be a threat, but she didn't want him to see what a pathetic mess she was.

Tex: So, are you good with that?

KitCat: Yes. Yes, I am. And will Melody be online, too?

Twice, Melody had joined them when Tex suggested talking to another woman might be a nice change for her.

Tex: If you'd like her to be. She said she's enjoyed talking to you. Pause. *And, KitCat? Just FYI. Don't tell her I told you, but she's been through her own hell, so she knows what it's like. Whatever is screwing up your life, she can certainly sympathize.*

Chatting with another woman seemed to be good for her. She hadn't done that for far too long. She'd given all of that up for her safety. Or maybe the fear that ruled her. She could try talking to his friend. If it didn't work, she could just avoid the chat room, although she'd miss it.

KitCat: Okay. That would be nice.

Tex: She can vouch for Quinn, too.

Good. That was good.

KitCat: So when will we do this?

Tex: How about tomorrow night? Nine o'clock okay? Or is that too soon?

She'd better get her shit together by then.

KitCat: That works for me. I'll be ready.

Tex: Chuckling here. He doesn't bite, KitCat. I promise you, whatever it is haunting you, he doesn't fit that mold.

KitCat: Okay. I trust you, Tex.

Tex: Good. We're friends, KitCat, and friends don't hurt or betray each other.

KitCat: I believe you. "See" you tomorrow.

His avatar disappeared, as did his name. Amy closed out of the chat room then shut down her computer and rebooted, just to be on the safe side. There was always a chance someone could hack into her computer despite all her safeguards. If only she could shut down and reopen her brain, maybe this fear would finally lessen. Ten years was a long time to let it keep a grip on her.

She leaned back in her chair and ran her fingers through her hair, dragging it back away from her face. It had gotten really long. She'd found a stylist who would come to her home, which was great, but she was overdue for an appointment. Maybe she'd call tomorrow. See if both the stylist and the security guard who came there when someone visited her home were available. A trim was definitely in order.

Not for Quinn Molloy, of course. He wouldn't even be laying eyes on her. No, just for herself.

Should she call Dr. Ybarra tomorrow and tell her what she was doing? Miracle of miracles, she'd found a psychiatrist who specialized in conditions like agoraphobia and made house calls. Yeah, maybe she'd do that. Get some feedback.

Okay. With two things on her to-do list, she made her way back into the bedroom and climbed into bed. Closing her eyes, she began the deep breathing exercises that Dr. Morrison had taught her to leave both her body and her brain. In seconds, she was asleep.

CHAPTER 2

Quinn Molloy stretched out his legs, paying careful attention to the one that would forever bear the damaging wounds. The one that killed his career with the SEALs. He made himself exercise faithfully, determined not to be any worse off than he was. Some days it was tolerable, but today it ached like a son of a bitch, a reminder of why he hadn't been able to get his shit together. If only there was some kind of exercise to get his brain fixed.

He blew out a sigh and wondered how the fuck he'd let himself be talked into this thing tonight. Talk to some strange female in a chat room? What the fuck? What was he supposed to say to her anyway? He'd pretty much lost all his conversational skills.

His leg might be marginally better but not his brain. He couldn't get the frightening images out of his mind, and he was certainly no fit company for anyone.

Dating was impossible, and he'd avoided almost everyone else he knew. Tex had survived a similar situation, although his was even worse. Quinn figured if he could find a way to fix himself, there was still hope for other things in his life. Maybe. He wasn't too optimistic though. Right now, he was hardly even good enough for himself.

His idea when he accepted the invitation had been to sit on Tex and Melody's back porch for a day or a month, however long they could stand him, contemplating his navel and the state of the world. The Keenans were each busy with their own things and assured him he could just hang as long as he wanted to. Melody said she'd be happy to feed him, but he'd have to do his own laundry.

He'd laughed at that last. He'd been doing his own laundry for as long as he could remember. And he could feed himself, if it came to that. Sometimes he cooked for Melody and Tex as a thank you. What he really needed was to be left alone so he could figure out if it was even possible to pick up the tattered fragments of his life. He'd had enough of death and killing and bloodshed. The last mission, the one that finished his career as a SEAL, he'd had to bury two of his SEAL teammates. That nearly did him in.

With the sun warming his face, he tipped his head back and closed his eyes.

"Alpha One, this is Alpha Two. Do you copy?"

It was hard to hear with the booming of guns all

around them, but Quinn pressed the headphones close to his ear.

"Go for Alpha One."

"Fuck, Quinn. They're all around us. How did this happen?"

"Don't know, buddy. You can bet I'll find out. Meanwhile, we need extraction. Hold one. I am coming to you."

He grabbed his HK MP5N submachine gun and crawled to where he knew Alpha Two was dug in. Heavy guns boomed all around him. A hail of bullets peppered the dirt right where he'd been crouching.

Shit, shit, shit.

He had just reached Alpha Two's position when he heard a scream and saw the last thing he wanted to see: two of his team members lying flat in the dirt, bleeding from multiple wounds.

"We gotta get out of here," Alpha Two—Brent Jakes—shouted at him.

"I already called for exfil. Let's make some noise so we can get these two guys out of here. Cover me."

As he crawled toward the two wounded men, a huge explosion sounded near them, and—

"Quinn?"

Quinn sat up so fast, he nearly fell out of the chair. His first instinct was to reach for his weapon, until he remembered he wasn't wearing one, so he reached for the throat of the person next to him. Strong fingers closed around his wrists.

"Quinn?" Tex repeated. "It's okay. You're here, not in the sandbox. It's all good, but what the fuck? Take it easy, buddy. You still having the nightmares?"

"Sort of." Quinn blew out a breath and shrugged. "Just bad dreams, okay?"

Quinn's heart was racing, and his hands were shaking. He wasn't back in the sandbox, he was in the home of a friend—who happened to be staring at him, one eyebrow quirked. He drew in a deep breath, forced himself to be calm, and sat up straighter.

"No, not okay. Been there, done that." He studied Quinn. "This happen a lot?"

Quinn shrugged. "Now and then. No biggie."

"Have you seen anyone about it?"

"I did the required headshrinker stuff before my discharge." He rubbed a hand over his face. "They'll go away, sooner or later."

"Take it from someone who's been there. It can be a bitch if you don't figure out how to deal with it."

Quinn didn't want to tell him that as a matter of fact, he hated closing his eyes at night. When he did, he could see his men, two of them bloody and dying as he and the others hauled them back to the exfil spot. His adrenalin was so high he'd barely even been aware of his own wound. They'd managed to keep them alive until the extraction, but they had both died back at the staging area.

Nothing had gone right with that mission. His lieutenant might have said a hundred times it was not

Quinn's fault, but he'd never believe that. He'd barely felt the pain of his own wounds, overshadowed as they were by the agony of losing those two men. The damage to his leg had been severe enough to earn him a medical discharge. He'd gone through physical therapy mostly so he could live on his own and not need someone to help him. Otherwise, he didn't give a shit.

He was as good as he was going to get physically but damaged in his soul and with absolutely no idea what he wanted to do with the rest of his life. Tex, who had overcome his own disability, had promised to help him, but talking to a strange woman online didn't seem to be what his mental health was looking for. He'd avoided women like the plague except for one incredibly intense weekend. Then he'd run without looking back, ashamed that he couldn't even recall her name. Was that what he was turning into?

Maybe he should call back that security agency that had been pursuing him. Even when he told them about his leg, they were interested in him. Something else he could either thank Tex for or curse him. In fact, Aubrey Reynold, head of the agency, kept telling him he had the perfect job for him right in Florida where they were located. A woman who'd suffered severe trauma ten years ago and had agoraphobia as a result so never left the house. Her real identity was a secret, and the agency did whatever her attorney asked to keep it that way. But it was a bad situation.

"Every time a stranger has to be on the premises, like a housekeeper or landscaper," he told Quinn, "I send one of my men over. His presence seems to make her feel better, but I'm trying to convince her she should have someone there full-time."

"In her house?"

"No. She's got a guest cottage out back. Not only could someone live there rent-free, they could also be getting a nice paycheck for doing it."

Quinn was actually tempted. He could hide away from people just like this woman was doing and serve a useful purpose at the same time.

"You know about my leg," he kept reminding the man.

"Not a problem. You won't be asked to do hundred-yard dashes."

Bringing it up always made Quinn feel less than a man, but, as Tex kept telling him, that was all in how he looked at it.

"This is a tailor-made job," he pointed out. "You'd be a fool to turn it down. And who knows what could come after that."

But he just couldn't seem to get to that point. Feeling sorry for himself was safer than trying something and discovering he couldn't do it.

Now he sat in the room Tex had set up as what Melody called computer central, finishing his coffee and wondering how crazy he had to be to agree to this. He'd only come here because Tex and Melody promised to leave him alone. Now they wanted him to chat online with some female who had her own problems? Fuck that shit. He was about ready to tell them he wasn't up for this when Tex nudged him.

"Come on, big guy," he teased. "Turn on your charm. A good lady can help chase the shadows. Ask me. I know."

Quinn shook his head. "I'm not sure I have any charm left to turn on. I have a feeling my shadows are here to stay, and I don't want to scare the poor woman to death."

"Yeah, about that." Tex rubbed his jaw. "She hasn't said, but I can tell from this and that she's got something in her past that apparently has scared the everloving fuck out of her. You know, the way she phrases her posts. Certain words she uses. Plus, she doesn't use her real name."

"How do you know that?" Quinn frowned.

"Because of what she calls herself." Tex chuckled. "KitCat. I figured it was a screen name. I asked her, and she said it's for the cat she has."

"Great," Quinn grunted. "So she's loony tunes on top of it."

"She's afraid of something," Melody reiterated. "I've read some of her posts and her answers to Tex and chatted with her a couple of times myself. Tex thinks she's afraid of something and really needs someone to talk to. I agree. And it does not make her crazy. I've been there, so I can relate."

“You think she’s being stalked like you were?”

“Don’t know.” Melody shrugged. “Whatever it is, though, I can hear myself in some of her posts. Afraid to even connect with someone for fear whatever is scaring you will use that somehow.”

Quinn blew out a breath. “Jesus.”

“Uh-huh. Tex swears he can tell by her posts that she’s got a core of steel under it all, but something has frightened her to death, and she won’t tell him what. He’s really good at reading between the lines.”

“Not that it’s any of my business,” Tex added, “but in some ways she reminds me of Melody when I first met her.”

Quinn’s eyebrow lifted. “Because she’s being stalked, or something close to it?”

“Not sure. Tex is the one who’s been chatting with her.” She looked at her husband. “Do you think that’s what it is?”

“Maybe.” He shrugged. “Maybe not, but something like it for sure.”

“And you got all this from discussing video game code with her?” Quinn had trouble hiding the skepticism in his voice.

“You know I’m good at reading people,” Tex told him. “Besides, sometimes we talk about other things. That’s the vibe I get from her.”

“So, exactly what is it I’m supposed to say to her to make her spill her guts?”

“No gut spilling, Quinn.” Melody shook her head.

"That's not what we want. We want her to connect with someone and maybe not feel the aloneness Tex senses in her." She grinned. "*Then* get her to spill her guts."

"The two of you are like little isolated islands," Tex added. "I just thought maybe you could share some kind of connection. She's designing this video game about SEALs. She wants information, and I figured you could answer her questions about them. It's not like you have to be in the same room with her, for crap's sake. The anonymity of the Internet is wonderful."

Quinn swallowed a sigh. He should just do this and get it over with. After all, Tex and Melody had been nice enough to offer him a place to straighten out his brain. It was the least he could do to repay their kindness. So, once and done and then he could get back to his own personal misery.

"Okay, but someone better get me a very large mug of coffee."

Melody blessed him with one of her incandescent smiles. "Coming right up."

"And don't blame me if I fuck this up."

She handed him his coffee and gave him a chaste kiss on the cheek. "Have a little faith in yourself. I think there's a real person underneath that grouchy bear exterior."

Tex seated himself at one of his many computers, and Melody pushed a chair into place on either side of him. She seated herself in one and nodded at Quinn to take the other. He'd connected a separate keyboard for each of them to make it easier for everyone to type messages. Quinn noticed the screen was large enough that all three of them could read whatever came up on it.

At one minute to nine, Tex logged onto the chat room. As soon as a kitten leapt onto the screen, he clicked on it and opened a private message box.

Tex: Hey, KitCat. How's it going tonight? Get that problem with the code fixed?"

KitCat: Oh, yes! Thanks so much. It's really moving along now."

Tex: Good. Good. Well, got some people here for you to meet."

Pause. Then…

KitCat: I'm not so sure about this, Tex.

Tex: Come on, you said you'd meet him. And, KitCat? I promise whatever you're afraid of, Quinn can chase the shadows. You have nothing to worry about where he is concerned."

Melody grabbed her keyboard.

Melody: Hi, KitCat, this is Melody. We haven't chatted in a while, so I thought I'd pop in. I just wanted to let you know that our friend is really harmless. We wouldn't want you to talk to him otherwise."

Tex nudged her, and she leaned over and kissed his cheek. Quinn tamped down the sudden surge of envy. Would he ever get his shit together enough to have that?

They waited for the other woman to answer Melody's post. Finally, a new message popped up.

KitCat: Hey there, Melody. Nice to see you again.

It was stupid to think he could get anything from anyone via the Internet like this, but Quinn was struck with the feeling that KitCat weighed her words and her answers very carefully.

Melody: Ditto. Pause. *We'll tell you anything you want to know about Quinn before you answer him, including swearing he's really trustworthy.* Another pause. I *say that because Tex worries that you might have some problems you're dealing with. Something he's sensed in your chats.*

There was another long pause, and Quinn wondered if they'd blown it. If the other woman resented what Melody had said.

Melody: KitCat? Sorry if I stepped on your privacy. That was not my intention. It's just that Tex is so good at sensing things in people, even over the Internet. And I promise whatever might be going on in your life, these guys can handle it and keep you safe."

For a long moment everyone held their breath. Then words began scrolling on the screen.

KitCat: Very nice to "talk" to you again, Melody. I want to tell you again what a great guy Tex is. He's helped me so much with my coding.

So she was just going to ignore the subject, Quinn thought. He could relate to that. But suddenly he had an urge to know exactly what was fucking up her life and if they could help. If *he* could help. And that shocked the hell out of him. What happened to his vow to be a hermit and stay the hell out of other people's lives?

While he was thinking, Melody pulled her keyboard closer to herself and began to type.

*Melody: There was a time he felt a lot more comfortable with strangers than anyone he knew. Don't tell him I said so, but you're right about him being a good guy. *wink* And here's another good guy we want you to meet. The one we told you about. Our friend, Quinn Molloy, was a SEAL, just like Tex. They don't come any better, take it from me.*

KitCat: I guess I have to take you at your word.

Melody: I promise you my word is good. She stopped typing and gnawed at her bottom lip. *My husband says you have a lot of questions about SEALs for the game you're designing. Quinn can answer them for you. He can give you the information Tex says you're looking for.*

Pause. Everyone waited for KitCat to make her next move. If she signed off, that was that. Then another message popped up.

KitCat: Okay. I guess I can give it a try.

Tex: Trust me. I wouldn't put anyone online with you that I didn't vet myself. He's definitely solid.

"Just answering questions," Quinn told them. "No personal shit."

He watched Tex and Melody smile at each other, and again he was tempted to call the whole thing off. He didn't want anyone thinking they could *fix* him. But KitCat's next message popped right up.

KitCat: Is he there now?

Tex began typing again.

Tex: He sure is. Say hey, Quinn.

Quinn centered his keyboard in front of him and took a deep breath. This was so far out of his wheelhouse he wasn't sure how to handle it, but okay. Maybe it would be better than wrestling with the dark thoughts that plagued him every night. He flexed his fingers and began to type.

Quinn: Hey, KitCat. This Quinn.

Now it was his turn to wait, wondering if she'd actually answer or just sign out. It was crazy, but he had this weird thought he could actually *feel* her through the Internet. Not her so much but her fear. Quinn knew about fear, but as a SEAL he was trained to face it and deal with it. He had a sense that with KitCat this went way beyond that. He was about to hand the extra keyboard back to Tex and forget the whole thing when words scrolled across the screen.

KitCat: Hey, Quinn. Nice to meet you.

Quinn let out a slow breath.

Quinn: Hi there, KitCat. I'd love to chat with you awhile. You good with that?

Another long pause.

KitCat: Sure. If Tex trusts you, I guess I can.

Tex pushed back his chair and stood, grinned at Quinn.

"You're good here. I think I'll go have a drink with

my wife. Come on, Mel. Let's get some grown-up time while the kids play.

Despite his teasing tone of voice, he squeezed Quinn's shoulder, a gesture that told his friend he was there if needed.

Quinn slid into the chair where Tex had been sitting, shifted his keyboard, and flexed his fingers. Okay, then.

Quinn: So what is it you do all day? Or night?

KitCat: Didn't Tex tell you? I design video games.

Although he had basic knowledge of computers, Quinn had never used them as a way of socializing. Truth be told, lately he rarely even used his laptop. He almost never sent email anymore, to the dismay of his friends and what little family he kept in touch with. Mostly he texted, and he did that from his phone. Short texts. Very short. He'd never been a touchy-feely kind of person and, with his life taking a sudden, abrupt turn, he was even less so. But now, odd as it was, at this moment, he found himself relaxing as he and KitCat rolled into their cyber conversation.

Maybe that's what his life was about to become, totally lived in cyberspace. Safer that way.

But don't forget. That's how Tex and Melody got together.

So what? That didn't mean it was going to happen here. To his way of thinking, that was a rarity rather than a usual occurrence. Tex, like himself, had shied away from personal contact except with his closest friends from the Teams.

Until he met Melody online.

Quinn: Video game? Sounds exciting.

He lifted his mug, took a sip of the still-warm coffee, and settled down for his electronic conversation. This was weird. He didn't know the woman, hadn't even met her in person, yet he felt this odd connection. Maybe that was the direction he should go since his social skills were so fucked up. Live his life online.

Okay, he'd better get down to business here. He'd promised to answer KitCat's questions, so that's what he'd do. He was just "chatting" with this woman and didn't even know her real name. And, for right now, that was fine with him.

Quinn: So tell me. How did you get in the video game business? And what's this game about SEALs Tex says you're designing?

CHAPTER 3

Amy leaned back in her chair and stretched her arms out, flexing her fingers. She could hardly believe two hours had passed while she "chatted" with a man she had just "met." Except for Tex, who had become an anomalous friend, she hadn't talked that much with anyone in what seemed forever. Of course, she hardly had contact with anyone, and, except for with Dan Rendell, had nothing much to say. She was always afraid either they looked at her as a weirdo because of how she lived or ignored her for the same reason. Even the security guards who came for brief periods of time.

But something about Quinn Molloy tickled her brain and woke up things that had long been dormant. After just over two hours, she felt as if she'd known him forever. She had a comfort level with him she'd never attained with anyone else, certainly not in the past ten years. And how odd that was. Maybe something was about to go right with her life, for a change.

She wondered idly what *Quinn Molloy* looked like. She'd wanted to ask him, but then he'd probably want the same details from her, and she wasn't ready to give out that information yet. Certainly not on the Web where anyone could steal it. She was 99 percent sure her computer was as hackproof as she could make it. She had done a lot of research and invested a lot of money in software to make it secure.

She tried to convince herself it was totally absurd to even worry about it after all this time. If someone was hacking into her computer, they'd already have done something about it by now, right? Certainly her conversations with him hadn't brought any unwanted intrusion. Besides, Tex wasn't associated with *him* in any way. She'd asked enough oblique questions to be as sure of that as possible. Her caution was born of the fear that even after all this time never left her.

Now she'd "met" Quinn, who at first seemed not quite as relaxed as Tex. Sort of uptight. Amy knew how he felt. If he was just back from a combat zone, he might be having nightmares like hers. But as they "talked," their messages became less stilted and, from the flavor of them, she could sense the tension easing in both of them. She had asked him questions about the SEALs, and he had been very forthcoming, if at times a little brief with his answers.

KitCat: Need to know, right?

Quinn: Something like that.

But that only whetted her appetite and made her want to find out as much as possible about this particular branch of Special Forces. Tomorrow, she told herself. Her brain was already tired from tonight. She stretched her arms out and cracked her neck, thinking she should make a cup of hot tea and use it to relax herself.

If only, she thought.

Lately, she'd been plagued by the nightmare again. Sometimes she went weeks without it. Then it would be back again, *boom*! She had no idea what triggered it, especially since Matthew was locked up tighter than a drum in prison. Right? She'd just checked again online. She should be immersed in the new video game coding, excited as she watched it come to life. Then why, for some unholy reason, had the really bad dreams begun to plague her again?

As if unable to help herself, she typed into the search bar the headline of *the* newspaper article, the one with all the details, and hit Enter. A few clicks of the mouse and there it was, in all its remembered gruesomeness. She hadn't read it for quite a while and knew for her mental health she probably should leave it alone. If only the nightmare would leave her alone. Tormenting herself this way didn't make it better, yet she couldn't seem to help herself.

Man goes berserk, kills family.

"Matthew Baker, the son of local financial adviser

Harrison Baker, without any seeming provocation, killed all the members of his blended family last night. His father, stepmother, half-brother, and stepsister were found viciously stabbed to death in the living room of the family home. A neighbor, hearing screams, looked out the window, saw a male figure fleeing the house, and called the police. She knew Matthew and identified him.

Police responding to the scene classified it as a bloodbath. "A scene that can cause nightmares," one of them told reporters.

Amy could certainly relate to that. Shuddering and suddenly nauseous, she clicked to close the document, swallowing the surge of nausea. She'd thought she could read it but had to stop after two paragraphs. Why did she keep doing this to herself, over and over again? The memory of her stepbrother screaming at all of them, the bodies of her parents on the floor, Matthew stabbing her, too, slashing at her. Thank god that was interrupted when Brian came into the room crying and asking what was going on.

She'd played dead and hoped he was done, but god, then he went after Brian. By the time she could find the tiny bit of strength to move and help her little brother, it was over, Brian was dead, and Matthew had run out the back door. Her brother's screams echoed in her ears for a long time afterward. To this day, she still believed there was a way she could have saved him, although she didn't know how. She was already bleeding out on the floor. Only the quick work of the EMTs saved her.

In the days following the massacre, everything was a blur. She was barely conscious when the EMTs arrived. The police, assessing the situation, had taken her to a hospital in another town and listed her under a false name. For days, she lay in bed, shrouded in pain and drugs and destroyed by the knowledge that her family was gone. She lived in a constant state of fear, terrified that somehow *he* would find her. Matthew. Her deranged stepbrother. The police did their best to assure her he believed she was dead. They convinced her she needed to stay that way or he might come after her again. The terror that never left her convinced her they were right. It meant she had to miss the closed-casket funeral for her family, and the overwhelming grief nearly destroyed her. But since there was a coffin for her as well, how could she have gone?

She still had no idea what had precipitated the whole thing. Although he had never quite settled into the blended family, he hadn't been distraught about it, either. Or so she thought. He was twelve years old when his father married Amy's mother. His behavior was always odd, and Harrison had problems dealing with him, but she and her mother had done what they could to keep peace. The two of them had never bonded, but that was okay. She knew a lot of families where even blood relatives didn't get along. She had her friends and now two parents instead of one.

Had it started when Brian was born, a child of the new marriage? Had Matthew been more angry, more uncontrollable? Did her parents chalk it up to the change in dynamics in the family? Amy just remembered how thankful she was to get out of the house when she left for college. The arguments and tantrums were becoming more frequent. That was when she quietly suggested to her mother that perhaps some professional help was needed.

That seemed to be a sore subject, so she left it alone, but she didn't come home much on vacations, either. This time, however, she had just graduated college and was visiting for two weeks before leaving for a dream job in Houston. Although Brian seemed happier, her stepfather appeared more worried and subdued than usual. Her mother, who now was tense all the time, told her quietly that Matthew had quit his job and stormed out of the apartment he'd been staying in. He had been gone for weeks with no contact with the family.

Had this been a regular thing while she was away at college and no one had discussed it? Amy had just been glad the few times she was home that he hadn't been around much or sometimes not at all.

"Harrison's really getting worried and trying not to show it," her mother shared with her.

Amy chose not to ask what had led up to the last break or why, after a month, the police hadn't been called to look for him. She just went about her business getting ready to leave and kept her mouth shut.

What had brought him back? And why had he killed everyone?

She still had only foggy memories of the weeks after the nightmare happened. It had taken every bit of inner strength and discipline to make the move from Texas to Florida and settle in the house. She'd be forever grateful to her father's attorney, Dan Rendell, who handled everything for her, including hiring people to help. But once she settled into the house, she seemed unable to set foot outside, as if Matthew would be waiting for her.

Now, ten years later, that bloodbath was still as vivid in her nightmares as if it happened yesterday, and she was still a prisoner in her home. She had made no friends here and certainly hadn't had a date. At this rate, she'd die without feeling the warmth of a man's body next to hers and the passion she wanted so badly. The miracle of children. The excitement of hot passion. All the things she'd dreamed of before the nightmare took over her life.

Why, then, could she not find the courage to break free of her self-imposed isolation?

She'd looked up the definition of agoraphobia when she was first diagnosed. She could almost recite it by heart. "A type of anxiety disorder in which you fear and often avoid places or situations that might cause you to panic and make you feel trapped, helpless, or embarrassed."

Yes, that was definitely her.

Dr. Ybarra explained with agoraphobia, you fear an actual or anticipated situation, such as using public transportation, being in open or enclosed spaces, standing in line, or being in a crowd. The anxiety is caused by fear that there's no easy way to escape or seek help if intense anxiety develops. That most people who have agoraphobia develop it after having one or more panic attacks, causing them to fear another attack and avoid the place where it occurred. In fact, she'd read, the fear can be so overwhelming that you may feel unable to leave your home.

That was her all right. Her first panic attack had occurred in the hospital. After that, they became a regular part of her life. She'd discovered she could control them but only if she never left the house. Or invited anyone in.

Sometimes she was so angry with herself, telling herself that after ten years the danger no longer existed. But, somewhere inside her, the fear wouldn't let go. Told her as long as Matthew Baker was alive, the danger was real. Not even Dr. Ybarra, the wonderful shrink Dan Rendell had found for her who came willingly to her home for their sessions, had been able to break down that barrier. After all these years, Amy was resigned to the fact she'd never leave her house again.

At least she opened the sliders to the patio so she could inhale fresh air.

Which was what she did now. Pouring a glass of ice water, she carried it into the family room and opened the glass doors. She stood there just a moment, letting herself settle into the rush of fresh air. A soft breeze drifted in, kissing her skin and ruffling her hair. It carried with it the scent of the periwinkles and Gerbera daisies and begonias that her landscape gardener planted and tended so carefully. She loved to look at them through the open windows and longed to stroke her fingers over the soft petals.

Then why don't I do it?

Then, after ten years of her self-imposed exile, a few times over the past month, she had actually managed to take one step outside to the patio. Inhaling the scented air and feeling the breeze on her face had felt so good. But then the panic gripped her again, and she'd quickly stepped back into the house, closing the door. Maybe she could try taking just a few steps outside now and see how that worked. Swallowing hard, she set one foot onto the covered patio then another and another. So far, so good.

Her heart was hammering so fast she could feel it in every pulse point of her body. Still, she was going to do this. She drew in a deep breath, let it out slowly and–

Wait! She froze in place. What was that noise?

She stopped, immobile. What was that noise? Just a whisper of sound, like a soft scrape of something. Was it the sound of a step? Was someone moving in her backyard? Impossible. She had a very expensive home security system. But then she heard it again. Just a whoosh of sound.

Suddenly, the heat of the agony in her arms and torso, the places where the knife had slashed her, burned through her. Remembered pain that had stayed with her all these years. Stepping back into the house so fast she almost tripped and fell, she slammed the glass door shut. As she did so, a night bird, probably startled by the loud slam, flew from a hydrangea bush and soared across the yard.

A bird! Of course! How stupid she was. How many times had she stood here over the years, willing herself to move forward, and seen birds flitting from bush to gorgeous bush, ruffling the leaves and flapping their wings. But never moving outside. Some might say the house was her prison. She saw it as a sanctuary. Even after ten years, she couldn't get rid of the thought that somehow *he* would learn she was alive and find out where she was. Stupid, she knew that, but there it was.

She had a top-of-the-line security system that included sensors everywhere. If anyone set foot on her property, alarms would sound both here and in the security company's offices. They were only turned off when the lawn service was working on her yard, and then she stayed in the house with the Glock .45 mm she'd bought. She had left the house only to learn to use it at a local gun range, and then she was accompanied by two well-armed and expensive security guards. Plus, it took a one-hour session with Dr. Ybarra before each trip to the range, and she was a wreck for hours afterward.

But she couldn't seem to get rid of the insidious fear that never left her. How was she ever going to get on with the rest of her life?

She closed the vertical blinds on the sliding doors, blocking out the world. Then stood there doing the deep breathing exercises Dr. Ybarra had taught her. She closed her eyes and visualized the calm waters of Tampa Bay, moonlight reflected on the water. Then she lifted the glass she was holding and drained it quickly, hoping the ice water would settle her.

Slowly, her heart rate returned to normal, and her hands stopped shaking. Refilling the glass, she carried it to the big chair she loved in the family room, curled up in it, and again took several deep breaths.

To distract herself, she switched her thoughts to Quinn Molloy. After spending two hours having an online conversation with the former SEAL, she couldn't help wondering what he looked like. Was he tall or medium height? Lean or heavily muscled? Did he have blond hair or dark? A beard? Scruff? Clean-shaven? Lord. When was the last time she'd fantasized about a man? Like, never? Oh, yeah, in college, before her world fell apart.

Their back and forth had been stiff and stilted at first, both of them testing the waters in an unfamiliar situation. She got the feeling he didn't live on the Internet the way she did, and that conversation didn't come easy to him. The only ones she'd had with men—with anyone, for that matter—had been with people like Tex who gave her technical advice. Okay, so she and Tex had become "friends," but he was married and safe. She'd shied away from everyone else, never sure who might be out there who could possibly be a friend of Matthew's and have somehow discovered her new identity.

She gave herself a mental shake of the head. No one could find her. Dan Rendell and the police had seen to that. Her tracks were well covered. And her obsessive checking on Matthew's status assured her he was still under lock and key. God! Would she ever get to the point where the openness outside her four walls would stop terrifying her? Where maybe, just maybe, she could have a real relationship with someone?

Of course, she wasn't sure she'd even remember how to act in that situation. That's why her online relationships were so much safer. But for the first time since that terrifying night, she had an urge, maybe even a craving, to meet someone face-to-face. Which shocked the hell out of her because where had that come from after a mere two hours of exchanging electronic messages with a total stranger?

Maybe she was losing her mind after all. Maybe she'd created a prison for herself, both physically and mentally, that she had no way to escape from.

Matthew's action had resulted in a jail situation for her as much as for himself.

At four thirty, she climbed into bed. Popped a tranquilizer and dozed off. But her dreams were filled with images of a mysterious warrior with dark hair, dark eyes, and a lean, muscular build that made every pulse in her body throb with unfamiliar need. She reached out for him, but the moment she touched him, he dissolved in a cloud of smoke, replaced by the image of a man holding a knife and covered in blood. Lips drawn back in maniacal hate, he took a step toward her, knife upraised, and…

She sat bolt upright in bed, eyes wide open, heart pounding so loud she could hear it. Perspiration covered her skin. Patience, who had awakened when Amy moved, mewed softly and curled into her lap. With a hand that shook so hard she had to make two tries at it, she switched on the bedside lamp and looked around, assuring herself the room was empty except for her. She reminded herself again that no one was in the house, or the security system would have alerted her.

And, of course, she had that Glock .45 mm she kept in her nightstand drawer at night and in the kitchen during the day. Sometimes she wondered if she should carry it around the house with her all the time. Then she'd have a tiny bout of hysterical laughter as she realized what her life had become and continued to be.

She blotted the perspiration from her face with the

hem of the sheet and tried to do the deep breathing Dr. Ybarra had told her would help. She also stroked Patience, the cat's purring a soothing sound. After a while, her heart rate slowed and her pulse stopped pounding so hard. She lay back down on the pillows but left the light on, sure she'd never get another minute of sleep that night. She wondered if she would be trapped in this prison of fear for the rest of her life.

But out of nowhere, she remembered the last thing Quinn had written after their unbelievably long chat: *If you have any more questions, I don't mind answering them.* Would Tex and Melody think it weird if she logged on tonight and asked for Quinn? And what about during the day?

Yes, maybe she'd see if she connected during the daylight hours. She might even feel like a normal person doing it that way.

CHAPTER 4

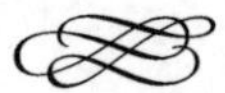

Bright sunlight filled the kitchen as Amy poured her orange juice. The sliding doors leading to the patio and the back yard were the only ones she didn't shutter or drape. Patience wound around her legs before going to stand by the doors, mewing softly.

"You want to smell the outside, baby?" Amy asked.

She was sure if she stepped outside, the cat would come with her, but their connection kept her in the house as long as her mistress was there. Maybe today she'd try it again. And hope another bird didn't scare her. Stupid to let a little thing like that frighten her, unless you were afraid of *everything* outside.

"Okay, my sweet kitty, let's give it another shot."

She pushed the sliding glass doors apart and stood in the opening, holding the glass of juice and enjoying the soft early morning. She could smell the scent of the lush flowers in her yard, the colors enhanced by the bright Florida sunshine. Patience wound her way around her ankles and rubbed against her as if telling her it was okay to step out.

Not for the first time, she was enormously grateful for the large inheritance she'd received. Between that and her fat royalties for her video games, at least money was not a problem. Dan Rendell had wanted to set up a corporation for her so she could market and sell the games herself, but she had nixed that. Such an arrangement would mean people to market the product, handle the sales, all those things. More people in her life, even if her anonymity could be maintained. She was happy with this arrangement. Between that and the income from her investments, she was able to live in comfortable solitude with solutions for all her needs.

Or had she made this a prison?

She had been chatting with Quinn Molloy for three weeks now—God! Had it been that long?—and the feeling she'd known him forever just kept growing stronger. Strange, since she'd never even met the man in person. But after the first week or so, when they'd gotten past all the questions about SEALs, the conversation just seemed to flow naturally. And that was weird also. She had never been one to put much faith in the success of coincidence, but she might have to reexamine that.

Somehow, they had moved smoothly from informational discussions to conversations about themselves. One time, Quinn told her how and why he had enlisted in the Navy and how he had tried out for the SEALs.

Quinn: It's a bitch. Ninety-five percent of the guys end up ringing the bell, telling the others they can't finish. I think I might be prouder of not doing that than anything else I've done in my life.

KitKat: That's why having to take the medical discharge bothers you so much. Right?

Quinn: You got it. I feel like a reject.

KitKat: From what Tex and Melody said, I'd think you were anything but.

*Quinn: *Snort* They have to say that. They're my friends.*

Another time he brought up the subject of where she lived and who with. She hesitated, not sure if she should give away her geographic location to a stranger. What if he was somehow connected to Matthew?

Please. How stupid was that? He was so far outside the realm of the type of person Matthew would be friends with that they weren't even in the same ballpark. Still, anonymity was her protection, and she clung to it like a perma-shield. Could she ever make herself let go?

Another time, they discussed activities they liked.

Quinn: What do you like to do in your spare time? You don't spend your entire life on the computer, do you?

*KitCat: *shrug* Pretty much.*

Quinn: I can't believe if there are red-blooded men where you live, they'd stay away from you.

KitCat: You don't even know what I look like.

*Quinn: *smiling* I have a good imagination. I think about the way you phrase things and try to imagine what the person saying them looks like. Of course, you could give me a rough description and put my mind to rest.*

That had stopped her for a few minutes. Once he had her description, he was another step closer to finding her, if he chose to look. Finding out who she really was. As farfetched as it was to imagine Matthew Baker out of prison and somehow fastening onto Quinn and then to her, she had learned anything was possible.

Quinn: KitCat? Even if you tell me you're built like a football player with a face like a boxer, it won't change my opinion of you.

KitCat: How can you have an opinion of me when we haven't even met?

Quinn: You don't think all these conversations are the same as meeting? Pause. *Come on. Give me something to dream about, okay?*

Dream about? Did he actually dream about her?

KitCat: You go first.

Quinn: Aw, I'm nothing to dream about. I'd rather have a description of you.

What could she tell him? That she was five foot five,

with long brown hair that she'd finally had styled again after too many months? That she hadn't put on a drop of makeup since she'd been squirreled out of the hospital? Yeah, not too many dream girls look like that.

She should cut this off before it went any further. After all, they had no future. She was locked away in a nightmare, and he needed to put his life back together. There was no future here. *She* had no future here. She was just a shell existing from day to day, checking obsessively to make sure the monster was still locked away.

But still, she kept up their conversations. It had reached the point where she'd be busy during the day, working on the new video game, and suddenly be struck with an urge to exchange messages with Quinn. She'd enter their private chat room, wondering if he was even at the computer, and sure enough, most of the time as soon as she posted a message, he answered. She asked him about that one time.

KitCat: Do you live with this laptop?

*Quinn: *grinning* Look*

KitCat: But I'm doing work!

Quinn: And I'm helping you with it, right?

She set up an alert in the private room so she'd know when anyone entered. These days, Tex seemed to have gone back to his own business, available if she needed him for technical advice but otherwise busy with his own thing. No, it was Quinn who opened that virtual door and called out to her. Mornings, evenings, the middle of the night. Apparently he slept as badly as she did. She actually found herself getting excited and anticipating their virtual meetings.

She often fantasized about his looks. She'd scoured every web site that even mentioned SEALs and downloaded enough pictures to fill an album. One night she spent three hours going picture by picture, enlarging the face of each SEAL and trying to imagine if that was what Quinn looked like.

But the most unusual—and unnerving—thing was that as time passed, he had begun to invade her dreams. Sometimes he looked like one of the pictures, sometimes another. She'd be standing on the shore, in her nightgown of all things, and he'd rise up out of the water and head toward her, arms outstretched. Then the image would dissolve and she'd be standing there by herself. And she'd wake up to discover herself sitting up in bed, arms outstretched.

She began to think she was really losing her mind. But at least it beat the nightmares.

Next time he was in the chat room with KitCat, Quinn was going to ask again, maybe find a way to coax it out of her. If she was afraid of something, did she have any protection? Was she hiding away in a tiny isolated cabin in the mountains or something?

"I was hoping whatever it is, you could coax it out of her," Tex told him. "People say you can't get vibes over virtual air waves, but I dispute that. I got them from Melody, and I was right on target."

"Well, she's not opening up," Quinn told him. "But I plan to keep trying."

"Just don't try so hard you push her away," Tex warned.

"Don't worry. I won't." He rubbed his jaw. "Is it weird to say you feel a connection with someone when you don't even know her name or where she lives or what the hell is going on in her life?"

Tex laughed. "You're asking the wrong person."

At two o'clock in the morning, restless and unable to settle down, he sat up in bed and opened the laptop. Maybe he could get her to at least answer one question. A few keystrokes took him into the chat room, and there she was.

Quinn: Waiting for me?

KitCat: meme of kitten flipping its tail

Well, well. Was she getting a little flirty? And was it the fact he hadn't had sex of any kind in months that made his cock suddenly hard as concrete?

Quinn: Will you answer one question for me?

Pause. He waited to see if she would close out.

KitCat: Depends on what it is.

Quinn: It's pretty simple. Will you tell me what color your hair is and whether it's long or short? I mean, hell, KitCat. I was on back-to-back missions then in the hospital for what seemed forever, and now hanging out with Tex and Melody. You're the first woman I've had any kind of relationship with in months. Give a guy something to dream about.

Pause. Had he lost her? No, she was still in the room.

KitCat: Dark brown. Long. And I don't do relationships.

Quinn: Thanks for that. Okay, I'll head off to bed and let you get back to work.

KitCat: Just like that?

Quinn: Catch you tomorrow. Or tomorrow night.

He backed out of the room. Maybe that would give her something to think about, enough that next time she'd answer a few more questions.

Closing the laptop, he slid down in bed, lying flat. Long, dark-brown hair, hmm? He closed his eyes and tried to call up some kind of image of her. He imagined her small and dainty, although he couldn't say why. There she was, in a flimsy nightgown, an image painted into his mind. She stood in moonlight. Her body outlined beneath the fabric of the gown. It brushed her full breasts and rounded hips. Her hair, brown like rich chocolate, drifted below her shoulders and framed a face he could barely make out. She walked toward him in slow motion, every movement so graceful it made his balls ache.

He'd been without a woman for a long time. There hadn't been one waiting for him when he was wounded, and he wasn't in the mood to look for one afterward. It depressed him that for so long he hadn't even had a hard-on. Nothing. He worried he'd lost his sex drive altogether, although truth be told he hadn't been much in the mood.

So how was it that a woman he'd never met in person, who obviously was tied up in a bunch of problems, was suddenly making him horny as hell?

As she walked toward him in the mist, he eased out of his boxer briefs and closed his fingers around his hot, aching shaft. With slow strokes, he moved his hand up and down, up and down. In his half-dream, KitCat lifted her nightgown over her head and tossed it to the side. Quinn's mouth began to water at the thought of nibbling at those ripe, deep-red nipples or sliding his tongue between her folds and tasting the sweet liquid of her sex.

Her cunt. Call it what it is. Her cunt.

Just the word sent the blood throbbing harder through the thick vein wrapped around his dick and made his balls ache. He imagined her lying beneath him, legs spread wide, imagined licking that cunt and tasting the nectar of her juices in his mouth. Sliding first one then two fingers inside her. Feeling that slick, hot flesh.

He eased his other hand between his thighs to cup his balls and stroked himself faster and faster.

She kept walking toward him, and when she moistened the tip of one finger and circled one nipple with it, his breath caught in his throat. He moved his hand faster and faster, up and down, up and down, squeezing his balls. He strained toward his climax, biting his lip to keep from uttering any guttural sounds and, god forbid, waking Tex or Melody.

And then, throbbing hard, he came, semen pulsing from the tip of his cock in a flood so thick and copious it flowed over his fingers and onto his wrist. He squeezed and pumped until he'd wrung the last drop from his body and the final spasm had subsided. He lay there, spent, exhausted, until the beating of his heart slowed and he could breathe somewhat normally.

Jesus Christ on a fucking crutch. How was it possible to have an orgasm that intense just thinking about someone who was only a figment of his imagination? He had to get to know her better. Had to find out what was screwing up her life that she was so afraid of seeing people or being seen, or telling anyone where she was. She was in his head now and his body. In his mind. Maybe he could convince her to confide in a man with a damaged body who wanted to protect her.

And make love to her. Hot, passionate love. To a woman he'd never even met. How screwed up was that?

Amy slept fitfully, her conversation with Quinn playing over and over in her mind. Why did he want to know what she looked like? It wasn't as if they were ever going to see each other. Right? Right? She was safe here. Matthew might be locked up, but who knew what the future would bring. If only they had given him the death penalty. But he'd had a top-notch attorney paid for with money she hadn't even known he'd had. As long as he drew breath, she'd live in fear.

Since the day she'd realized it was only a bird that had scared her in the yard, she'd tried standing in the open sliding door again a few times. Patience always stood with her, tail wound around her legs as if offering assurance that there was nothing to be afraid of. She had no idea what she'd do without the cat who gave her unconditional love and seemed to sense when fear overtook her.

She still heard the same noises every time she opened the door, but she always forced herself to remember what it was and swallow her fear. A bird. Just a bird. Maybe by next week she might actually have the courage to take her juice or coffee out onto the patio. Possibly when the landscape people came to do her yard and Dan Rendell's security guard was there to make her feel safe.

Sometimes she thought how stupid it was that she needed an armed guard to protect her from the landscaper or housekeeper or whoever. After all, the same company and many of the same people had been doing her yard since she'd moved in. Ditto for the housekeeping service she used. And Dan, who continued to be her only human anchor to the world, always vetted any new people hired by either company. The last change had been with the housekeeper three years ago but again, she'd been assured both by the company and Dan that all the woman's credentials had been checked backward and forward.

She was so thankful that Dan had stuck with her all these years. Of course, she had him on retainer, but not everyone would have been as patient with her as he was. He was really the only constant in her life and did so much more than oversee the management of her money. She'd cut her visits with Dr. Ybarra down to only occasional sessions since it didn't seem like they were getting anywhere, even after all this time.

She managed to keep her loneliness at bay reading, watching movies, and working on video games. In fact, the video games had become a lifesaver. She could lose herself in the creation of them and forget about how and why she'd ended up this way. Not even Tex had made her want to change things up. But now she'd been "talking" to Quinn for three weeks, and she found herself wondering again what he looked like and how he was in real life. Because electronic life was far from real. It was just safe.

Quinn was great about answering her questions relating to SEALs. But then, as if it was the most natural thing, they'd gotten into other topics like movies and television programs and favorite foods. One night turned into another and another. After that first night, she'd logged on every evening at nine Eastern Time—Was he in the same time zone?—and there he was, without even Tex or Melody as a buffer. Yet somehow, with him, she felt safe. She was aware that was stupid. She didn't know him, really. But after she'd learned Melody's story about being stalked, she decided if they trusted Quinn, she could, too.

Still, the day after Tex had "introduced" them, just in case, she'd called Dan Rendell and asked him to check Quinn out. The man had been in the military, so there'd be records. When he called to tell her Quinn Molloy was not only squeaky clean, he was a decorated SEAL whom the military spoke of very highly, she actually relaxed.

"And talk about coincidence," he added. "Security Solutions, the agency we use for you, offered him a job. He's looking for a place to live. Amy, this could be the perfect solution for everything."

At first her knee-jerk reaction had been to sever all connection with him. She liked the anonymity of their relationship. If he met her, he'd probably think she was the queen of the weirdos. Then she thought, could this be the one person she'd finally get up the courage to meet in person? She didn't count the people who cleaned her house and did her yard or maintenance work. Times when Dan always sent a security guard any time one of them was there, just in case. What if she had protection here all the time?

Protection from what? she asked herself. Matthew

was locked away. It was herself she was hiding from. Still…

Maybe one of these days she'd get up the courage to meet Quinn in person. A real live contact after all these years. The idea of him taking the job with Security Solutions actually intrigued her. But what if he met her and ran as far as he could in the opposite direction? How did she even do that? Or what if he turned her down without so much as meeting her? Then she'd lose their electronic conversations.

She had a sudden urge to connect with him right now. Glancing at her watch, she saw that it was nine thirty. What was he doing now? She had no idea of his schedule. Did he go out by himself? Maybe she'd just log on and see if by some chance he was hanging out in the private chat room, hoping she'd show up. They always hooked up at night but maybe…

She filled a mug from the single-serving coffeemaker and carried it into the room where her computer was. As soon as she sat in her chair, Patience jumped up, settled herself in Amy's lap, and began purring. When she first moved into the house, Patience had shown up from somewhere. One of the security guards had scoured the neighborhood, but no one seemed to claim ownership. And Patience didn't seem to want to leave. It had worked out well, the two of them bonding and providing comfort for each other.

She took a sip of coffee, set the mug down on the mug rug on her desk, and woke up her computer.

Before she could talk herself out of it, she logged on and entered the private chat room.

KitCat: Quinn? You up early today?

A very long minute ticked by, and she was about to sign off when his message popped up.

Quinn: Early? You kidding? This is late.

KitCat: What time do you get up? I thought you stayed up late at night.

Quinn: I told you. I don't need much sleep. What about you?

Pause.

KitCat: Neither do I. Really. Sleep is highly overrated.

Quinn posted a grinning emoji.

Quinn: Sounds like we have something in common.

KitCat: Where's Tex? He's usually at his computer by now, from what he says.

Quinn: He's working. He set me up with this laptop. So, what do you do during the day besides design video games?

KitCat: Not much. Read. Watch movies.

Quinn: Not even just hang out with friends?

Amy stared at the screen. Every normal person had friends, right? So what should she do? Lie? Tell him the truth? He'd think she was a raving lunatic. But just maybe she could share a little with him. Dan had given him the seal of approval, as had Tex and Melody. Security Solutions wanted to hire him. So what was holding her back?

What if she told him a little about herself and checked his reaction? She had to admit that while she'd resisted full-time security all these years, having Quinn living in the guest cottage would make her feel a lot better. But just him. No one else.

Lately, she'd been having weird feelings where Matthew was concerned, even to checking the prison site two and three times a day. She was suddenly overcome with a need to share things with him and check his reaction.

She'd carried the burden for so long.

Quinn: KitCat? Still there?

KitCat: I'm here.

Quinn: So, tell me about your friends.

She began typing before she could second-guess herself.

KitCat: I don't have any friends.

Pause.

Quinn: ????????????????

KitCat: It's a long story.

Quinn: I've got nothing but time and a good ear to listen.

He had shared some of the details of his nightmares with her. Could she do any less? She felt as if her brain was frozen.

Quinn: You still there? Ready to tell me that long story?

Was she really going to tell someone she'd never met the horror story that was her life?

KitCat: Not yet.

Quinn: You have to be ready at some time to face it and unburden yourself.

Dr. Ybarra had told her the same thing over and over.

"I tell you," she'd pointed out.

"Not the same thing."

Suddenly, her courage deserted her. Maybe next time, she told herself.

CHAPTER 5

Amy pushed away from the computer and went to refill her coffee mug yet again. No wonder she hardly slept. She was overdosed on caffeine. At least it left her with fewer hours to wrestle with nightmares. Sleep was becoming another stop on the road to hell.

The words of her last conversation with Quinn played over and over in her head.

Quinn: You can tell me whatever it is. I've been through hell myself.

KitCat: Not like this, I bet.

Quinn: I'll take that bet. I've seen enough slaughter and mayhem to last three lifetimes. I'm right there with you.

KitCat: How do you deal with it?

Quinn: Not easily. I didn't want to accept help, either. If not for Tex and Melody practically dragging me here, I'd still be a basket case.

Pause.

Had he gotten tired of her and signed off? She couldn't say she blamed him.

KitCat: You still there?

Quinn: I am.

Pause.

KitCat: I guess I just don't want you to look at me different than you do now.

Quinn: Why don't you give it a shot and find out?

Another pause while she sat there chewing her lip. She guessed she wouldn't be any worse off than she was now. But first she wanted something else. Maybe if she could "see" him she'd feel better.

KitCat: I want something else first.

Quinn: Name it.

KitCat: You answered very fast.

Quinn: Because I want you to have whatever makes you feel comfortable. So go ahead. Ask me.

She inhaled slowly and blew out a breath.

KitCat: You asked me what I look like. I want the same from you. I want a photo of you.

Quinn: A photo?

Amy could almost hear him shouting across the ethernet.

KitCat: Nothing fancy.

There were Share buttons in every chat room in case the people talking wanted to exchange photos. She waited a long time for Quinn's answer, about to tell him to forget about it.

Quinn: Okay, but you have to do the same.

Oh god. Could she do that? Break the wall of privacy that shrouded her? What if someone else got hold of this photo? Could she trust Quinn with it? As if reading her mind, he broke in.

Quinn: I promise on my honor as a SEAL that the minute after I look at it, I will destroy it. Shred it into tiny pieces.

KitCat: Can I trust you?

Quinn: I hope so, but if you can't, no harm, no foul. I'll just keep working on it.

The worst part was she wanted the picture of him badly, and she'd come to believe she could trust him, Strange, right? Trusting a man she'd never met.

KitCat: Okay.

Quinn: I'll go first.

Amy watched as the Share button wiggled on the screen, there was a flash, and then a photo of him stared her in the face. Holy mother of god, he was a wet dream walking. And she hadn't had a wet dream in so long she wasn't sure she even remembered what they were. He was wearing jeans and a dark T-shirt and leaning against a seawall. His sculpted muscles pressed against the fabric of his clothes and spoke of hours and hours of rigorous training, not to mention the type of things SEALs did on their missions.

But it was his face that captivated her, lean with an angular jaw, high cheekbones, dark eyebrows, and hair that looked black cropped close to his head. So, he wasn't one of those guys who took advantage of relaxed dress regs and let his hair grow long. She knew Special Forces had exemptions in a lot of areas because of the covert missions they participated in.

Yes, he was a hottie, with the kind of smoldering good looks that captivated women and made them want to tear his clothes off. Other women, of course. She hadn't wanted to tear a man's clothes off since before the night of the bloodbath.

Don't think about that. Focus on Quinn.

She was still studying it when another message scrolled across her screen.

Quinn: Did I scare you silent?

She gave herself a mental shake.

KitCat: Not at all. In fact...

Quinn: In fact, what?

KitCat: In fact, some women might say you are actually good-looking.

*Quinn: *grinning* Some? Not you?*

KitCat: I don't want you to get a big head.

Ohmigod, was she flirting with him?

Quinn: I'm restraining myself from making dirty remarks here because I want to see a picture of you. Let's have it. A promise is a promise.

Amy swallowed a sigh and pushed back the feeling of trepidation surging through her. She only had one picture of herself on her personal computer, a selfie she'd taken recently so Dan Rendell could update his files. He wanted to make sure that anyone he sent around to her house knew what she looked like just in case.

No. Forget just in case. It hadn't happened and wasn't going to. She'd just have to keep telling herself that. She clicked on the icon in the chat room and pulled in the photo, one of her sitting in a chair in her living room. Before she could change her mind, she clicked it into place. And held her breath. What if…

No. She trusted Tex and so she trusted Quinn.

KitCat: So, what do you think?

Quinn: Wow! That's all I can say. Wow!

KitCat: Wow? I guess that's good. Right?

Quinn: Damn straight. I'll definitely be dreaming about you tonight.

Oh god. What had she done? She didn't want him dreaming about her or any other thing. Still, it had been ten years since she'd flirted with a man or felt his touch or shared a kiss. *Had sex!* And out of nowhere, although the fear that lived with her was still there, she wanted something more with this man. She wanted to feel human. Like a woman.

As if, she thought.

But then she typed a message before she could think or take back the words.

KitCat: So that means I can dream about you, too, right?

Quinn: Damn straight I hope you do. And I hope that doesn't scare you off.

She paused while she tried to find the right words.

KitCat: Quinn, I have a huge problem, and I know if you knew what it was, you'd run as far and as fast as you could.

Quinn: Try me. I'm a SEAL. Nothing scares me.

KitCat: This would turn you off altogether.

Pause. What was he thinking?

Quinn: Tell you what. You sleep on this. Then you check me out. You can find anything on a computer. Quinn Molloy. Look for anything you want. Then tomorrow, whenever you're ready, come meet me in our chat room. I hope you'll be ready to share your secret with me then.

God. Could she? She'd held it inside her for so long, but just maybe…

KitCat: Okay. See you tomorrow.

She signed off before she could say anything she shouldn't. Then she sat back in the chair and wondered just what she was getting herself into.

Quinn was up early in the morning. His clock read six when he sat up in bed. Less than four hours sleep, yet he didn't feel tired. Was it because he'd dreamed about KitCat again? She puzzled him and intrigued him, but something else was niggling at the back of his mind. She had no friends. She lived alone. She had suffered some kind of trauma that had transformed her life.

He wasn't a big believer in coincidences, but he never disregarded them. He wasn't very religious, either, although he did believe in god. And when coincidence happened that changed his life for the better, he wondered to himself if god was watching out for him.

And he was wondering if the element of coincidence was at work in his life again. Was KitCat like the woman in Florida who Security Solutions wanted him to protect, or was she, in fact, the actual woman? He could ask her but then he might frighten her away.

Take a chance? Not take a chance?

Fuck, Molloy. Do it or forget it.

He couldn't hang out at Tex and Melody's forever.

Hauling himself out of bed, he took care of his bathroom chores, fetched a mug of coffee from their single-serve coffeemaker, and carried it with his laptop out onto the porch. The sun was coming up, bathing everything in the gold of early morning light and making the colors in the foliage even more vivid. It was a peaceful scene, which was good because that was what he needed right now. Peace and calm.

He turned on the computer and logged onto the private chat room. This would be a sign, he told himself. If she was there this early, he'd lay it out for her. If not, he'd rethink the whole situation. Either way, it would be a sign.

He had no sooner logged into the private chat room than he saw the little kitty cat prancing across the floor.

Yes!

Quinn: Up early, KitCat.

KitCat: You, too.

Quinn: Had stuff on my mind.

KitCat: You, too?

Quinn: Wanna tell me what's on yours?

KitCat: You go first.

Pause.

Quinn: Do you believe in coincidence?

KitCat: Depends. Sometimes. Why?

Quinn: Before I answer, let me tell you a little more about myself.

*KitCat: *chuckle* I thought you already did.*

Quinn: Only the bare essentials. You know I joined the Navy right out of high school. Two years in, I tried out for the SEALs and made it the first time.

KitCat: Wow! I'm impressed. Besides what you told me, I've been readin' up on them. Only a tiny percentage ever graduate from BUD/S.

Quinn: That's right. I'm proud of that and my career as a SEAL. And I say this not to brag but because I want you to have the full picture. I served with honor and even collected a few medals, although that's not why I did it.

KitCat: I believe you.

Quinn: I only left because I was injured and not fit for active duty any longer. But I can still do a lot of other things.

KitCat: I know you can, but where is all this leading?

Quinn: Just bear with me. I can't run as fast as I used to or do some other things, but otherwise I'm in good shape. And I've been offered a job.

KitCat: Quinn!!!!! That's fantastic. What kind? Where? Are you taking it?

Quinn: That depends.

KitCat: On what?

Quinn: On you. Please answer this question and don't be scared and log off. Do you live in Florida?

Her answer was so long in coming, he was sure he'd frightened her to death and she'd logged off.

Quinn: KitCat? You still there?

Finally her answer scrolled across the screen.

KitCat: Why do you ask?

Quinn: Because Security Solutions offered me a job protecting a woman who sounds just like you. I was wondering if this was the best coincidence of my life.

Another long pause.

KitCat: I checked you out.

Yes!

Quinn: Good. I was hoping you did.

KitCat: Did they tell you my story?

Quinn: Only the bare essentials. I'd rather hear it from you. If you want to tell me, that is.

Quinn: I wish I was there. I'd hold you and soothe you and show you there's nothing to be afraid of.

KitCat: But...what if there is?

Quinn: What do you mean?

On the other end of the conversation, Amy sat with Patience in her lap, her heart beating so fast she was sure it would jump out of her chest. Was this a sign telling her things might take a turn for the better? That she had someone who could make her feel safe? What if he got here and didn't like her after all?

But then, as if a movie trailer was unfolding in her brain, she saw how much of her life she had lost. The thought of what Matthew had stolen from her along with everything else made her physically ill. For the first time since that horrific night, she was filled with the desire to kill Matthew Baker for what he'd done to her and her family. Everyone else was dead, and she might as well be, for the kind of life she was living.

Tell him, a voice deep in her brain whispered. You know you want to.

And she did. For whatever unexpected reason, she wanted to get the words out. If it chased him away, if he decided not to take the job, well, she hadn't really lost anything. Had she?

Amy drew in a deep breath and let it out slowly.

KitCat: I'm going to send you a link to something. After you read it, if you want to stop talking to me or not take this job, I'll understand.

Quinn: What do you mean?

KitCat: Just read it.

She pulled up the article and copied and pasted the link into her message then hit Send. Her coffee had cooled by that time, but she didn't care. Lifting the mug, she took a healthy swallow, making a face at the bitter taste.

Unable to sit there while he read the article, she nudged Patience off her lap and went to refill her coffee mug. Standing at the sink, she blew on the steam rising from the liquid then took a tiny sip. She wondered after reading the article if he'd think she was a freak. He was smart enough to realize she was the daughter everyone thought was dead. But then what?

She walked back to her desk with slow steps, Patience trotting beside her. When she sat down, the cat jumped into her lap again and curled up against her, as if knowing she needed that special comfort. She'd have to tell him about the agoraphobia. She had no idea if Security Solutions had mentioned that. Would he just decide she was a screwed-up pain in the ass with too much baggage and not take the job?

Finally, she set her mug down and tapped her mouse to wake up the screen. And stared at Quinn's message.

Quinn: That's as bad as anything I've seen in combat, and I can tell you firsthand, shutting yourself away doesn't make it get better.

KitCat: So you say.

Pause.

Quinn: My last assignment I saw two of my team members killed in front of me, shredded by bullets. I was injured, too, which is how I got the medical discharge. I'm out of the service, and I've been through rehab, and I still can't get rid of the nightmares. That's the main reason Tex and Melody insisted I get my ass down here and hang with them for a while.

Oh my god! She stared at the screen. How awful for him.

Patience, sensing her distress, made little mewling sounds and did her ecstatic kneading.

KitCat: How are you doing now?

Quinn: Getting there. Being with Tex and Melody has helped ground me. So, what do you think? About the job?

Pause.

Quinn: Don't get scared and run away. You can trust me. I can't believe you've been trying to handle all this alone. Don't you have anyone to help you there?

KitCat: My wonderful shrink and the fantastic attorney who has been my anchor all this time.

Quinn: I figure the shrink lives in the area, but does the attorney?

She shook her head before realizing he couldn't see her.

KitCat: No. He's in Texas.

Quinn: KitCat, that's why you should have someone close by in case you need them. And not just a stranger to whom it's only a job.

Her pulse accelerated again.

KitCat: Are you saying it's more than that to you?

Quinn: Damn straight. That okay with you?

Her palms were sweating so she wiped them off on her jeans and began typing.

KitCat: Um, yes. I know it's stupid but I keep thinking, what if Matthew has a friend who's been searching to see if

I'm really dead? What if even now he has people searching for me?

Quinn: That takes money. Does he have any? And how would he use it without anyone catching on?

KitCat: I don't know. This is probably irrational, but I've lived with the fear for so long I keep imagining all kinds of things.

Quinn: And when I get there, we'll talk about them. I might even have good old Tex get on the job. He can find out anything about anyone.

Amy actually smiled and began to type again.

KitCat: So you're taking the job? Are you sure? We don't even know each other.

Quinn: Listen, KitCat. I haven't been the most sociable person since my discharge but stupid as it may sound, I feel some connection here. I want to do this, if it's okay with you.

Should she take a chance? She hadn't been with a man in any way, shape, or form for ten years. Or anyone, for that matter, except the help and her shrink. But hadn't it just been today she'd gotten angry at how isolated her life was? At the shambles she'd made of it because of Matthew?

KitCat: I have to tell you something that maybe Security Solutions didn't make you aware of.

Quinn: Okay. Anything you want to tell me I want to hear. Nothing can scare me away, all right?

KitCat: I hope you mean that because this story would scare away just about anyone.

Quinn: Not me. I'm a SEAL, remember?

Okay, then. She took a deep breath and plunged right in, telling him about her agoraphobia, shocked she was even admitting it to a stranger. Once she got started, it was as if she couldn't stop herself.

Telling him details about her mother's second marriage, about Matthew and the tension and disruptions he caused was bad enough. But when she got to the details of the night of the massacre, her fingers were trembling so much she could hardly write.

What did he think now? Would he even answer her or just disappear without even signing off? She wanted to cry. If she lost this connection, she'd be back in that isolation chamber where she'd lived before they "met" online. Did that mean she was ready to deal with the fear? Had she made a tenuous, unexpected connection with Quinn? She hadn't thought about a man in *that* way—in *any* way—since that horrific night. How weird that on the basis of a few weeks' worth of online conversations, she suddenly yearned for something else.

Patience, sitting in her lap and apparently out of the quality she was named for, began meowing and doing ecstatic kneading on her thighs. It was enough to jerk Amy back to the present, which then drew her attention to a new message on the screen.

Quinn: At eight thirty, I'm calling Security Solutions. As soon as I have details, I'll get back to you. Maybe if you have full-time security, and it's someone you really trust, the other problem will get better. I really want to help you with that.

So, uh, KitCat, do you have a cell phone, and are you comfortable giving me the number?

She answered before she had time to outthink herself.

KitCat: Yes. Here it is.

She typed it out for him.

KitCat: You'd better give me yours, too. I only have five numbers programmed in. Everything else is blocked.

Quinn: Good idea. Okay, here it is. The numbers popped up on her screen. *Okay, back shortly.*

She hoped he meant it.

CHAPTER 6

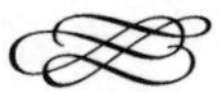

Matthew Baker lay on his bunk, stretched out full-length, resting his head on the hands clasped behind it. For someone who had been in prison for ten years and was faced with no change in his status, ever, he was unusually relaxed. He was just glad no one could see inside his head.

Not that they hadn't tried. From the moment he'd been caught after what he'd discovered was a massive manhunt. He had kept his mouth shut. He had told his attorneys he would plead not guilty and that was all he was saying. He told the shrinks they kept throwing at him he had nothing to say to them. Period.

After all, what could he say? That he'd killed everyone because they pissed him off? Even though that was the truth. For as long as he could remember, even as a small child, a rage had burned inside him. His mother had kept it at bay by coddling him and giving in to his whims and temper tantrums. But then she died, and dear old Dad, had never understood him or had patience with his volatile nature. Just expected him to toe the line, like other kids his age. But he wasn't like other kids, and his father either never understood it or never wanted to.

When Harrison Baker remarried, the rage at some woman taking his mother's place had set him off on his first killing spree. He had been fourteen at the time, but sharp and devious for his age. He simply skipped school for a day and hung out in the seedier part of the city, viciously stabbing anyone who pissed him off, but doing it out of sight of others.

Then he had put on an act for his father that should have won him an award, calling the old asshole and telling him he'd skipped school because he missed his mother so much and could someone come and get him. He even made nice to the bitch his father had married, shedding crocodile tears and hugging her even as he controlled the overwhelming desire to cut her heart out.

He was smart, which was how he had managed to operate on the fringes of the family for all those years. The bitch of a stepsister he'd acquired made him the angriest. She was such a prissy, Miss America piece of crap, but his father, who had wanted a daughter since Matthew's half-sister disappeared from their lives, thought she hung the moon. Matthew just wanted to hang her from a rafter.

Things got a lot worse when Brian was born. Harrison and his stepmother now hung all their hopes for an outstanding son on him. How many nights had Matthew stood in the nursery, clenching his fists to control himself and keep from strangling the brat. By the time Brian was nine, Matthew had had it. He was living in the apartment they'd built for him over the garage, with its own entrance, although many nights he didn't come home at all. When he finally couldn't stand it, after one screaming match too many, he'd left, finding a place on the other side of the city.

Good old Harrison, probably trying to ease his own conscience, set up a trust fund for him when he kicked him out of the house. Oh, sure, some of this might have gone for his defense attorneys, but there was still a fat bundle left, even after the farce of a trial. He had opened a numbered account before he was arrested, in one of those phony offshore banks, with the one person in the world he trusted. That way no one could check to see if any of the money was used. By anyone. No one but he and his friend could find it. The only other person with access. Matthew might be crazy, but he was also crazy smart.

And he knew how to make that money grow each time he took it out and then found an even more lucrative source. Selling drugs, with the one friend he'd made. The one person he trusted. He had plans for that money, and the one person in the world he could trust was going to help him achieve his ends.

But first, he had to get out of this fucking prison. He'd studied everything about the place, the building, and the guards and planned carefully. Tonight was the night, and all it had required was some of his constantly growing stash of money and the work of the one person he had trusted for years. And of course, a lot of patience.

For ten years, he had called on that patience, reliving that night over and over. Sometimes the images excited him so it was as good as sex. He could close his eyes, his hand wrapped around his cock, and experience a release more intense than any actual sexual experience. He was becoming so aroused now he was almost tempted to take himself in hand, but in a few moments his entire life was going to change and he needed to be ready.

He decided he'd save it all for his stepsister. He'd never believed the police when they told him she was dead. When he stabbed her, he was in such a fucking rage and wasn't sure in his own mind if those wounds had been fatal. Too bad. She was the ultimate cause of all his troubles. He remembered lifting his hand with the knife to finish her off when that pissant brat Brian had come into the room and started crying and yelling at him. Shit, it had felt so good to stick that knife in the scrawny little chest. But the rage that had driven him there had eased enough, and he knew he had to get the hell out of there.

And he knew where to go. He had plans to make

because there was always the chance he'd be caught. And sure as fuck it happened. He was. Caught, tried, convicted, and locked away. But he still had his secret weapon, his one and only friend who had already begun the campaign for him. In a few minutes, he'd be in position to put his entire plan into action. Then he'd have his real vengeance.

Lying on his bunk, he smiled. He could hardly wait.

His time was coming.

* * *

Amy could hardly sit still, impatient for the minutes to pass. She checked her watch and the clock on the computer at least a hundred times.

She figured Quinn would not be able reach anyone at Security Solutions until the office opened since this wasn't an emergency. Be patient, she told herself. But after ten years in hell, she didn't have much patience left.

She'd wanted to tell him about her uneasy feeling, but maybe she could do that when he got there. And maybe he could give her some advice that would make her feel a little better. She just hoped when he was confronted with it in person, her agoraphobia didn't scare him off.

All the articles she'd read about the disease, all the things Dr. Ybarra had discussed with her, all boiled down to one thing. The agoraphobe was the only one who could take control of the situation, but it took an incentive to do it. Was Quinn going to be that incentive? Could it happen that fast? She had an instant trust with Tex and then Melody, and they had vouched for Quinn. So had Dan Rendell, and he wouldn't have been offered this job if he hadn't checked out. Right?

Meanwhile, she paced and chugged coffee until she was on a real caffeine high.

At eight thirty, when she was about to scream from tension, her cell rang. She grabbed it up and pushed Talk.

"Quinn?"

"The one and only. Okay, I have info."

"Just tell me when you'll be on your way."

He chuckled. "In a few minutes."

Her eyebrows nearly hit her hairline. "How? What—"

"I made contact with Chuck Deland at Security and got a big go-ahead from them. He said your attorney will be overjoyed."

Amy could just imagine. "I'm sure he will. So, can you give me details?"

"Sure." Quinn cleared his throat. "As soon as I hang up I'm going to pack. Security has a helo on the way, and Tex is driving me to the pickup site. It's only a little more than an hour to when we land. Security says they'll have a vehicle for me." He paused. "They said you don't have a car."

"That's right," she agreed. "If you don't leave the house, you don't need a car."

"Okay. Well, I'll have a GPS plus written directions. I'll call you the moment we land. And Security says they're sending someone to your house now to hang out until I get there."

"Hang out?" She frowned at the phone. "Why?"

"I'm told Dan Rendell had coincidentally asked to step up your security."

Amy's stomach clenched. "Is— Is something wrong?"

"Not that I know of, but we want to make sure it stays that way. Also, their agent will have my credentials and check me out to make sure I am who I say I am."

"Now you know why I like them so much," she pointed out.

"And why I'm taking this job. By the way, can I ask you one question before we hang up?"

"Uh, sure. What is it?"

"How about telling me your name? Although I guess I could keep calling you 76KitCat."

She actually giggled. She didn't remember the last time she'd done that, even though she was about to rip away the curtain she hid behind.

"It's Amy. Amy Ressler. At least that's the name I've gone by for the last ten years."

"Amy?" She heard a touch of humor in his voice.

"No wonder this was meant to be. Melody's best friend is named Amy."

And suddenly, that little bit of information made her feel better, as if this whole complex connection was actually meant to happen.

"I guess that's the frosting on the cake," she told him.

"Listen, I have to get packing and finish up some stuff here. Then Tex is taking me to wait for the chopper, but I'll see you very shortly. The flight's less than two hours plus travel time to your house."

"See you then."

Hurry, she wanted to tell him, filled with a sudden sense of urgency.

* * *

Matthew Baker closed his eyes and forced himself to relax. It was almost time. Messages had been sent and received, and all the arrangements had been made. It was amazing what could be accomplished when you had money. He was just so fucking smart, hiding everything in plain sight, in a way that didn't draw anyone's attention to it. And his additional source of income? Still operating smoothly as long as he had his secret weapon to help him. His secret weapon, right under everyone's nose.

His plans were already in place. Again, money had greased the wheels getting messages back and forth and setting things up. He'd have to be careful at first. There'd be too many eyes on the situation. But he'd waited this long. He knew how to be patient. Living in this hellhole for ten years had taught him that.

Mental discipline was what it took, something he hadn't learned until after the fact. But now he had it. In spades. He could spend his one hour a day in the yard with the vermin he was shut up with and pretend he was anywhere else while putting on a well-behaved show for the stupid guards. He was back eating in the dining room with the other inmates after he'd learned the hard way that his temper tantrums got him no place.

He'd learned a discipline he'd never had before and how to use his brain properly. He actually managed to get library privileges and used the scarce amount of time they allowed him to research different ways to kill people, painfully. The stupid idiots had never caught on.

And he'd received information that the fucking stepsister was still alive. He knew it. He just knew it. He had to admit they'd done a masterful job of promoting the myth. For a while he'd almost believed it himself. But he still remembered those last few seconds when he was killing Brian, and the memory of her arm twitching and reaching out. He'd had to make sure, and his secret contact had done so for him.

He had plans for her, and he was more than ready now for that and everything else. All of it. He could hardly wait. He was lying there running everything through his mind again when the guard rapped on his cell.

"Okay, Baker. It's time."

* * *

When the phone at the gate rang through to the house, Amy was sitting at her work computer, the laptop that had the camera feeds sitting to her left. She was always careful to carry it into whatever room she went to, and plug it in so the power didn't die and leave her with a blank screen. Looking over now at the laptop that monitored the cameras, she saw the familiar face of one of her regular Security Solutions agents. They'd become almost like members of the family over the years, if she had a family. Which she didn't.

She pushed the Talk button in the intercom on the wall.

"Hello, Agent Grillo."

She supposed she could call them by their first names by now, but the formality was another form of protection for her, a shield against letting her guard down.

"Good morning, Miss Ressler. The office informed you I'd be coming today?"

"Yes, they did. Do you have any further updates on Mr. Molloy's arrival?"

"I do. The helicopter has landed, and he is on his

way here from the facility in one of the agency vehicles."

She knew the agency, in addition to its offices, had a separate building where they kept two helicopters, off-road vehicles, and other paraphernalia. She had been too frightened at leaving the house to take the tour they'd offered her, so Dan Rendell had arranged for a video version. She'd thought it extremely impressive and applauded Dan for using such a powerful firm.

"Thank you for letting me know."

"If you'll open the gate, I'll pull in and wait for him, rather than sitting in my car out on the street."

Of course, dummy, she told herself. Sure. Leave him out there to call attention to herself. She was well aware the agents had remotes that could open the gates if necessary, in case of an emergency, but they always waited for her to do it when possible. It was a small measure of control that made her feel a little more secure and also made her appreciate the respect they gave to a nutcase like her.

"Thank you so much. If you'd please let him in when he gets here and then let me know on the intercom, I'd be very grateful."

"Absolutely. And if there's anything else you need, just let me know."

"Thanks again."

She watched on the laptop as the gates opened and a black SUV drove through and up the curved driveway to the circle in front of the house. The property was not that wide—land was obnoxiously expensive in South Tampa—but it was deep, which meant there could be lots of mature foliage to provide as much of a screen as possible to anyone watching from the street.

Agent Anthony Grillo pulled up and parked in the curve of the circle, leaving room for Quinn with whatever he was driving. Amy knew that at the office they would have given him the code for the side entrance to the garage as well as a special remote.

In an uncharacteristic action, she hurried into her bedroom and raked through her closet, looking for something to wear that didn't look like Little Miss Mouse. Too bad for her that she'd gotten rid of all those clothes. Damn. She finally settled on a pair of slim jeans and a short-sleeved blue T-shirt that had a cat embroidered on it. One of her rare indulgences. She didn't keep makeup anymore, but she did have a tube of lip gloss. She changed in a hurry, released her ponytail and brushed out her hair, and swiped on some lip gloss. A glance in the mirror told her she wouldn't be getting calls for photo ops, but she figured she was passable. After all, this wasn't a date, right? Then why was she so nervous?

She hurried back into the kitchen and checked the clock on the stove. Fifteen minutes had passed. How long now until he arrived? She tried to avoid looking at her watch every ten seconds, and she certainly didn't need any more coffee. Her nerves were already jangling. Patience, true to her name, sat on the kitchen counter and reached out her head to rub against Amy's arm, her own recipe for soothing jangled nerves.

"We're going to have someone moving in with us, Patience," she told the cat, stroking her ears and forehead. "Well, not quite in with us. He'll be in the cottage."

She'd come further than she expected in such a short time, but she wasn't quite ready for someone actually to be living inside the house with her.

Patience mewed at her.

"Yes, baby girl. You'll get to put your stamp of approval on him, too."

While she was waiting, she called Dr. Ybarra, who asked a million questions, of course. Then, apparently satisfied with what she heard, she asked Amy to call her the next day and let her know if things were working out as she expected.

"He could help you with your breakthrough, Amy," the psychiatrist said. "If you trust him, embrace the situation. I'm crossing my fingers for you."

She tried not to pace after she hung up the phone, but the seconds seemed to crawl by. At last, the doorbell rang. She checked the camera feed at the same time she heard Agent Grillo's voice coming from the intercom.

"Miss Ressler? Agent Molloy is here."

Agent Molloy! After their conversations, she had a hard time thinking of him as anything but Quinn.

"Good. Please have him park in the garage and then bring him into the house."

She watched on the camera feed as Quinn opened the garage door and pulled in the vehicle he'd been given, a black SUV like the one Grill had been driving. She wondered a little hysterically if their entire fleet was like that.

Hands clasped together nervously, she waited in the kitchen until the door to the garage opened. Agent Grillo entered first, and right behind him was the man she'd been waiting on edge to meet. She noticed when he walked in, the limp he'd told her about, but it wasn't anywhere near as bad as he'd led her to believe.

Please let this be good. Please let it work. Please, please, please.

Quinn Molloy was at least six feet tall, lean and muscular like his pictures, with the kind of scruff beard that looked good on her favorite actors. His black hair was longer than in the picture he'd sent her, but she figured he hadn't had it cut since the shot was taken. High cheekbones balanced out a square jaw in a face that looked almost stern and forbidding. His midnight-black eyes, framed with thick black lashes, were laser-focused directly on her and a shiver raced down her spine.

Damn. Maybe this wasn't such a good idea.

But then he smiled at her, and she felt bathed in unexpected warmth. And strength. Security. Safety. Feelings she hadn't had in more than ten years. That sense of connection she'd felt when they were chatting online came walloping back, and, for the first time since that horrendous night, she felt safe. The tension in her body eased, and even her almost-dead hormones were pushing and shoving to get out.

"Hello, Amy Ressler." His voice was deep, but he spoke softly. "Or should I call you KitCat?"

Her body relaxed, and she smiled back at him. "Amy. Please."

He took a step forward and held out his hand. "I'm very pleased to finally meet you."

His hand was slightly rough but warm, his fingers firm when he wrapped them around hers. At his touch, a bolt of heat shot through her, a feeling so far in the past that for a moment she didn't recognize it for what it was. God! She'd actually had any kind of sexual response to a man for the first time in ten years. She didn't know whether to be frightened or thrilled.

She realized he was waiting for her to say something.

"Um, I'm happy to meet you at last, too. Thank you so much for doing this."

Agent Grillo cleared his throat. "I thought I'd show Quinn the security camera setup and the monitor. Then I'll give him the rundown of the guesthouse and make sure he has all the codes he'll need. I'll let the office know everything is okay. Then I'm taking off, if it's okay with you, Miss Ressler."

Amy nodded at him. "Absolutely. Thank you for making this happen."

"Our pleasure. I can tell you the agency is happy to have Mr. Molloy on staff now. Both the boss and Mr. Rendell believe he's the best person for this job."

"You know I'll be doing my best." He spoke to Grillo, but he was looking at Amy. "I think we're good here." He winked at her. "Right?"

"Yes. Absolutely." She even felt her lips curve in the unfamiliar shape of a smile. "Thanks, Agent Grillo."

Grillo looked from one to the other and grinned also. "My pleasure."

She watched through the sliding glass door while Quinn toted his luggage and what looked like grocery bags to the guest cottage, Grillo showing him the code for the door and handing him the backup remote. A few minutes later, they walked back outside, shook hands, and Grillo took off for his car. Quinn disappeared for a few moments back into the cottage and, when he reappeared, he was holding two take-out food containers. She managed to open the sliding doors for him then stepped away. He entered, closed the slider behind him, and set two fresh food containers on the counter.

"One of the things they told me in the briefing is you don't like that door open. When I called Dan Rendell just now to let him know I was here, he reminded me of it, too."

For the first time since his arrival, she felt embarrassed by her situation.

"I'm sorry. It's just that I can't—"

"No problem." He took her hands in his again, the touch of them so reassuring. "I want whatever makes you comfortable. That's the theme of the day." He nodded at the counter. "I thought I'd bring lunch for us. I don't know what you like to eat, but I'm hoping these will appeal to you. I got a fresh salad and a great sandwich. We can split them if you like."

"Thank you. That was very thoughtful. I, um, noticed that you stopped and bought groceries on the way here. I, uh, would be happy to feed you."

God. She sounded like an idiot, stumbling over her words. And where did that offer to feed him come from anyway? She hardly even cooked for herself. Every month she had meals to freeze delivered from one of the restaurants she liked, and Publix delivered her groceries. Since *that night* she hadn't had much interest in food anyway. Now she was offering to cook for someone?

"Sounds nice, but for now I'll feed you." He winked. "And if cooking's not your thing, Melody says I'm not half bad in the kitchen. Meanwhile, how about showing me the laptop where the cameras feed into. Then, let's have lunch."

She snapped herself out of her trance, and they carried the food to the breakfast room table. She added plates, silverware, and napkins then paused at the refrigerator.

"I don't know what you drink. I don't have beer or anything, just water and iced tea. I'm sorry."

He shook his head. "No need to apologize. Iced tea would be great. And just FYI, I never drink alcohol of any kind when I'm on a mission."

She paused in the act of getting out glasses. "Is that what this is? A mission?"

He was at her side in an instant, taking her hands again.

"It is, but I hope you know that it's much more than that to me. *You're* much more than that to me." His thumbs caressed her knuckles. "I have so much I want to say to you, but I don't want to scare you the hell away and make you fire me."

The unaccustomed smile played over her lips again.

"I do, too. Have things to say to you. I'm just so afraid that you'll decide this is a big mistake and tell Security Solutions you can't do this."

He shook his head. "Not gonna happen. We'll take it one step at a time, but I promise I'm not leaving."

She blew out a breath. "Thank you so much for taking this job."

"This is more than a job. Okay? So get that out of your head. We're going to fix this. All of it."

"That's a pretty big order. I'm kinda a hot mess, and I have been for a long time."

"But with good reason," he pointed out.

"Would you believe me if I said I think I'm losing my mind? If I haven't already lost it, that is."

"No sweat. Been there, done that." A buzz sounded, and he pulled his cell phone from his pants pocket, looking at the screen. "Mr. Rendell wants me to call him and give him my assessment of the situation. Let me get that out of the way."

"You can make the call out on the patio," she told him. "I'm long past having the desire to know any of the details of everything. Unless he's calling to tell me Matthew Baker is dead, it's nothing I need to hear."

"Sounds good, and thanks for being so accommodating about it. Then how about we sit down and share some lunch. Are you working on your project this afternoon?"

She shook her head. "I'm taking the afternoon off."

"Good. After we started talking, I began doing research on agoraphobia. You know, Amy, it's really not as rare as you think. Maybe we can even find a solution that will help you live a normal life."

She blinked away the tears welling in her eyes, stunned that he'd done such a thoughtful thing. But god, she hoped he was right.

"Okay. I think I am ready for that. More than ready."

CHAPTER 7

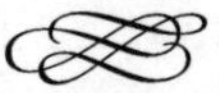

"How the fuck did this happen?"

The moment he'd received the phone call, Dan Rendell had flown by private helicopter to the prison where Matthew Baker had been incarcerated. Just when he thought things were looking up for Amy, with the arrival of Quinn Molloy, her increased security, and her trust in the man. He'd hoped that this was the beginning of an uptick in the quality of her life.

Now he stood in the warden's office with the district attorney who had prosecuted the case, the head of the US Marshal's service who had been keeping tabs on the woman living under the name of Amy Ressler, and Bobby Abadelli, the lieutenant in charge of the shift when Matthew Baker managed to ghost his way out of the prison. He couldn't remember the last time he'd been so enraged. He glared at Warden James

Forrest, barely restraining himself from pounding on the desk.

Forrest, whose face was a pasty gray at this point, looked as if he wished he was any place but here. Instead, he slid his gaze to Abadelli.

"Bobby? This was your shift. Who the hell was in charge of that wing?"

Abadelli didn't look any too happy himself. "Ian Fletcher. Jim, he was in charge of that wing because he's been here eight years and has a good record. He puts the fear of god into the inmates. They might hate him, but they also respect him because he doesn't take shit from anyone."

"So, what went wrong tonight?" Rendell demanded. "This isn't the kind of prison people can just slip out of."

"We're working on it,"Forrest assured him. "Fletcher seems to have disappeared right after he took a group of three prisoners to the showers. One of the officers went to check when he was doing a walk around and noticed three of the inmates on that wing were missing. He checked the showers, found two of them out cold and Baker in the wind."

"And no Fletcher," Marshal Doug DeMarco pointed out.

"No Fletcher," Abadelli agreed. "I've got men scouring the prison for any sign of him, but I'd say at this point he's in the wind as well."

Rendell snorted. "No shit."

"I contacted Washington on the way here," DeMarco told him. "My boss is already getting a nationwide manhunt underway. We have people and procedures in place so we're ready for this, unfortunately." He sighed. "Even though we always hope we won't have to use them."

"Good, good." Rendell blew out a breath. "Now. Everyone pay attention. I want a complete lockdown on all of this. Total silence. Not a word leaks out of here to anyone. You threaten your men with castration, Forrest, if they so much as breathe one word to anyone. Especially the media."

The warden nodded. "I'll take care of it. Abadelli can help me. He's the best lieutenant I've got."

"Listen. I've got to call Security Solutions and give them a heads-up. I also want them to start digging and see if they can find anyone connected to Baker we don't know about. He had to have outside help on this as well."

"You should suggest having someone assigned there twenty-four seven," DeMarco said. "We might also need to think about relocating her, at least until this asshole is caught. I've already got people looking into alternatives." He shook his head. "I can tell you, she's not going to be happy. Just getting her out of the house and into a vehicle is going to take medical assistance. She'll never make it out the door without some kind of tranquillizer."

“She’ll be a lot less happy if she’s dead,” Forrest pointed out.

Rendell shook his head. “That may not be necessary.”

“What do you mean?”

“I always think it’s funny how timing is everything in life. Apparently she struck up an online acquaintance with a former SEAL, someone she ‘met’ through a source she uses for questions on the video games she designs.”

“A stranger?” DeMarco’s tone was sharp.

“Yes and no. They’ve been chatting for almost a month. But rest assured, when she met him, she sent me his name right away, and I had everything about him checked out, including who his kindergarten teacher was. And Security Solutions already had him on their radar. They hire a lot of former Special Forces.”

“So he’s solid?” DeMarco asked.

“As granite. He’s taken a job as her twenty-four seven on-site security. That in itself is unusual because she hasn’t let anyone in the house for ten years except for contract work and then always has at least one agent on-site.”

“That means she’s protected.”

Rendell nodded. “But I have to pass this information along to him. He needs to be on full alert. I just don’t want her to find this out yet. She deals with enough psychological problems as it is. Maybe we’ll get lucky and catch him right away, and she'll never have to know."

DeMarco nodded. "Understood. But you know there are no guarantees."

"I do. That's why I'm also going to tell them to keep him off the books. I don't know who's helping Baker or what kind of resources they have. I'm sure Baker already knows all about her existing situation, but I want to keep Quinn as our secret advantage."

"Good idea," DeMarco agreed.

At that moment, the phone on the warden's desk rang, and he grabbed up the receiver.

"What is it?" The last vestige of color faded from his face. "Where? Okay. You know what to do. Get it done." He dropped the receiver into the cradle. "Fuck, fuck, fuck."

"Now what?" Rendell asked.

"We sent four guards to search the perimeter outside the prison to see if we could find traces of anything. Someone had to get Baker out of here and off the prison property, and there's only so many ways you can do that. The guards just found Fletcher's body about a mile down the road, next to his abandoned car."

"So he's dead," DeMarco said.

"Christ." Abadelli raked his fingers through his hair, his face as pale as the warden's. "I would have bet my life on him being one of my best. He's been with us eight years."

"Money does weird things to people," Rendell reminded him. "Baker has a very fat bank account, which his father set up when he kicked his son out of the house. Soothing his conscience, I guess. I've never checked on it. Had no reason to until now. I'll have to see if it's been touched and who would have had access to it. As far as I know, all his acquaintances were slimy individuals, and he had no close friends."

The warden nodded. "He never had even one visitor in prisoner. Even our worst inmates get a guest now and then."

"I'd say it was deliberate," Rendell told him. "You can bet he's been planning this since the day he became an inmate here. He waited until he thought he'd be off our radar and didn't want to leave anything for us to follow."

"This would have to be someone he really trusted," DeMarco pointed out. "We never turned up anyone when we were doing all the background checks before we moved Miss Ressler. It's going to take a lot of digging to find out who that is."

Forrest sighed. "I'd say we need to do a thorough checkup of all the prison personnel. Someone's been paid to smuggle notes or whatever in and out. Maybe even a cell phone." He pounded his fist on the desk. "God damn it. Running a place like this is hard enough without having to worry about your people being corrupted."

"That's the damn truth," DeMarco agreed.

"I'll help," Abadelli told him. "You know you can trust me, and you can hire someone to check me out if you want to."

"Good idea," Rendell agreed then glanced at his watch. "I'd better get on this right away." He looked at each of the men in the room. "You all have my office number, my private line, and my cell. I want to be kept in the loop on every single thing, no matter what."

"Where will you be?" DeMarco asked.

"My office as soon as I get back, doing a video conference with Security Solutions. Then Florida if I think it's necessary. I just want to try to handle this without scaring the shit out of her." He looked around. "I don't want any of you to contact Amy about this."

"No worries there," DeMarco assured him.

"And one more thing." He turned to the warden. "She's obsessive about checking to make sure Matthew Baker is still listed as imprisoned. Do not put this out in the records where she can check it out. That's an order from whoever needs to give it."

No one offered any objections and, with one more look around, he stormed out the door. There was one thing he had to do right away. Call Quinn Molloy who was now installed at Amy's house.

* * *

Per his instructions, Jamie had used a chunk of the money Matthew had transferred to buy a car. Not a new one, but only slightly used and intelligently selected. Matthew would have preferred a black utility vehicle. He thought of them as symbols of power used by the Secret Service and many security agencies, both public and covert. He entertained an image of himself being driven around in one of those. He'd be dressed in a black suit, black tie, and black aviator shades, with a Kimber .45 mm in a shoulder holster. He'd pick a spot frequented by the kind of people he hated, people like his late bastard father. Jamie would pull up to the curb, he'd walk in, pull out his gun, and start shooting at will. Then, while everyone was still in shock, he'd be back in the vehicle, and Jamie would drive them away.

To the next location.

People had dissed him all his life. Now he wanted to show them who had the power. Who could decide who would live and who would die. Jamie seemed to find the idea exciting but kept reminding Matthew he had a job to do first.

As if he could forget.

It wasn't bad enough his father had married that stupid bitch to begin with, completely forgetting Matthew's mother and his other unknown offspring. And he all but *ordered* Matthew to treat her with respect and do his best to help the cohesiveness of this new family.

Co—what?

Fuck that shit.

He wanted his own mother back, who thought he

hung the moon and let him do whatever the hell he wanted, despite his father's rantings.

The new wife had been just a tight ass, who didn't want him to have any fun. She had *rules*, for fuck's sake, and he was expected to follow them. And the princess? Another tight ass, a simpering one. He wanted to pull out every hair on her head and mark her face with cigarette burns. His stepmother went out of her way to make sure they were never alone, especially after she caught him up in the tree, peering into her bedroom window. Damn. She never let him have any fun.

He thought—hoped—that when he stormed out of the house that last time his weak sister of a father would finally stand up for him, but he hadn't even bothered to try and contact him. Instead, he'd had his high-priced attorney call Matthew to tell him a bank account had been set up for him with substantial funds so he wouldn't be broke, but he was to stay away from the house.

Well, he showed them. He'd found a way to turn that money into ten times what he was given then had his revenge on his so-called family. Nights in prison when he couldn't sleep, he'd think of all that blood and the bodies and get so hot he'd jack off with the image in his mind.

In any event, the car Jamie bought and picked him up in was an innocuous dark-gray sedan. In the back was a suitcase filled with the clothes Matthew had requested be purchased. He could hardly contain his exuberance as they drove away from the area of the prison.

"We need to put a couple of hundred miles between us and the prison before we stop for the night," he told Jamie. "Then we can look for a place to stay. You know what I want."

Jamie nodded. "Not on the main highway, preferable some midsized town. No sweat. I scoped some unlikely areas out the past couple of days. I didn't want a place on the interstate, and I wanted to stay away from small towns. All places where we might stick out like a sore thumb."

Matthew nodded. "Good thinking. So what did you find?"

"A mid-priced hotel in a midsized town that caters to people on the road. If they happen to be full up when we get there, there are three others in the same city."

"Perfect." Matthew grinned. "I always knew you were smart."

It was close to midnight by the time they got to the hotel. Jamie handled the check-in then parked the car in the small adjacent garage. They could take the elevator to the second floor and enter the hotel without going through the lobby.

"A shower," Matthew said as soon as they were in the room. "A real shower with honest-to-god soap and nobody watching me. Can we get some food?"

"Uh-huh." Jamie tossed some take-out menus on the little table. "Just tell me what you want."

In the bathroom, he stripped off the jeans and T-shirt he'd changed into in the car, dropping them on the floor and turning the shower on full force. He stood under the stream of water for a long time, soaping his body three times and rinsing off before he was finished. At last, he turned the shower off and reached for a towel, slowly drying himself off. God, what a pleasure that had been. He'd spent ten years enduring group showers three times a week with little-to-no privacy. He was sure no matter how long he stood under the stream, he might never feel clean again. And the best part? There was no one watching him. A close second was the freedom to stand beneath the spray for as long as he wanted to.

"You still alive in there?" Jamie called from the bedroom.

"Still breathing, despite it all."

He stared at his face in the mirror, leaner than ten years ago and bearing scars from prison skirmishes. But, in the end, the other prisoners learned not to mess with him. His hair, black with some strands of early gray, hung to his shoulders. He needed to cut it, erase the prison look, because he knew by now the news was out and the cops—all the cops—were searching for him. He was probably number one on everyone's list. He just wasn't sure which photo they'd be using—then or now. Well, a little hair dye would help, too. He'd keep the moustache but ditch the beard.

He wrapped the towel around his waist and walked out of the bathroom. Jamie had shopped for him so he had clothes, but he wasn't in the mood to get dressed now. He just wanted to sit and revel in the fact he was free before he had to step into another personality to do what he'd been waiting ten y,ears to accomplish.

"It's about time." Jamie was sitting at the small table in the room, arranging two large pizza boxes and some paper plates and napkins. "I can't believe with all the choices available, the food you want the most is pizza."

Matthew laughed, something else he hadn't done for a long time. "It is amazing the things you miss and want when you can't have them. For me, one of them is pizza."

Jamie laughed and lifted out a slice of the pizza. "I would have thought the thing you missed the most was sex."

Matthew winked. "Not as long as I have my good right hand. Let's eat and talk."

"I have to say your exit was plenty smooth, just as you predicted. When the guard gave me the message and told me where to meet you, I thought you were having pipe dreams."

Matthew just smiled. "It worked like a charm. Too bad he won't be around to enjoy the fruits of his labor. You got the money to his widow?"

Jamie nodded. "Just like you said."

"Good. Couldn't leave him around to give us away, but I didn't want his wife to suffer."

Jamie almost choked on a bite of pizza. "Since when are you such a caring person?"

"I always pay my debts," he said in a solemn voice. "But sometimes we have to improvise."

"You know they're already looking for you."

"Let 'em look. I know how to be invisible."

"And they'll be staking out the little prissy's house."

"Don't worry. I plan to get this done and not get caught. I'm not going back to prison."

"Okay, okay. I believe you. Just as long as you don't rush into it."

Matthew glared. "I am done rushing into things. That's how I ended up where I am now. Okay?"

"Yes. Okay, okay. Just making sure." Jamie took a large bite of a steaming slice, chewed, and swallowed. "So, what do you want to know?"

"You tracked her down? For real? I mean, this is not some big joke on your part because I'll tell you, I'm not in a laughing mood where she's concerned."

"Would I lie? I'm the only one who always tells you the truth, remember?"

"And thank god for that." He took a swallow of the beer that sat at his elbow. "Okay. Tell me about it."

"First, it took all these years because the person who arranged this did a damn good job of it." Jamie barked a laugh. "Would you believe it? I even dug up the grave and pried the casket open. With help, of course. Empty, just like my source said."

Matthew frowned. "I hope you put it back the way it was."

"We did a good job," Jamie assured him. "Count on it."

"That better be the truth." He gestured with impatience, wanting to know everything. "So, then what?"

"It took a lot of chasing and a big chunk of your money." Jamie waved the hand holding the slice of pizza. "But I did it. First of all, she's changed her name. No big surprise, after all, but I got past that. And I tracked her down. She's living in Tampa. Bought a big house there in the rich section of town." He added in a conspiratorial tone, "The best part? She never leaves there."

Matthew lifted an eyebrow. "Never?"

"Nope. Seems what you did scared the shit out of her. I think she has what's called agoraphobia. Yeah, you really frightened her." Jamie chuckled.

He smacked his fist on the table. "I knew it. I knew she wasn't dead."

"You can find out anything if you have enough money," Jamie pointed out.

"And she should be scared. As soon as I get my hands on her I'm going to hack her to death piece by piece. Stupid little bitch. Miss Priss Goody Two Shoes. She ruined everything."

Jamie shrugged. "If you say so."

"You should feel the same way," he snapped. "She had the old man wrapped around her skinny little fingers."

"I'll get mine when she's dead."

"So, tell me about this place where she lives."

"Matt, you can't go there right now. It's the first place they'll look for you."

He nodded. "I know. I just want the details. You went there? Scoped it out? Took pictures, like you said you would?"

Jamie nodded, chewed a bite of pizza, and swallowed.

"Okay. For one thing, it's like a fortress. A high wrought iron fence around the entire property with a very sophisticated security system. Plus, when the housekeeper comes to clean or the landscaper to do the yard, she usually has a security guard on duty."

"What about packages being delivered?"

"Get this. She has them delivered to the office of the security agency she uses and one of the agents brings them to her. The only exception is Publix Supermarket that delivers her groceries."

"She doesn't even go to the supermarket?"

"Huh-uh."

Matthew snorted. "I must have done a good job if she's still scared shitless after all these years." He took another swallow of beer. "But that makes it harder to get to her."

"You think I've been idle?" Jamie scowled. "I've used

your money to the best advantage, and we have a number of options. None of them easy but all workable. We just have to analyze each of them and see which fits."

"I want to know all about the Publix deliveries. That might be a possibility. And I want to scope out the neighborhood."

Jamie lifted an eyebrow. "I think it's chancy. You'll have to wear an excellent disguise."

"That's another way that having money helps," he pointed out. "I can buy any kind of disguise I want."

"Are you sure I can't talk you out of waiting a while? At least until the initial furor over your escape dies down?"

"Not a chance. I'll disappear afterward while we make plans, but I want to take a look at her neighborhood now."

"So, let's finish the pizza, get a good night's sleep, and hit the road."

He winked. "Sounds good to me."

CHAPTER 8

Amy studied Quinn as he chewed the last bite of his sandwich. What pleasure she got from just watching him. Everything was done with an economy of movement, even eating. Everything appealed to her from the flex of muscles in his jaw to those in his arms. The black T-shirt and jeans he wore made him look even more like a warrior, but the edge was softened slightly by the scent of whatever aftershave clung to him.

Aftershave? With a scruff beard? Oh, right. In all her research for her video game characters, she'd learned that there were special razors and clippers that could be used to keep that style of beard neat and clean. She wondered what his body looked like beneath the jeans and T-shirt. If he had a fat stomach, washboard abs, a tight ass—

Tight ass? Holy crap? What the hell was wrong with her? Was she going crazy? Maybe it was the fact she hadn't had sex in ten years, or even the desire to dream about it. Although after Quinn had sent her his picture, she'd been on the verge of a few fantasies about him.

"A penny for them." His deep voice broke into her meanderings.

She blinked. "Excuse me?"

"You looked like you were deep in thought, and I wondered what had such a hold on your concentration."

If only you knew.

Heat crept up her face in a very unfamiliar blush, and she lifted her ice water, taking a long drink. Hoping it would cool her off. She felt like a teenager whose hormones had just escaped confinement.

"Um, it was nothing. Really." *Please believe me.*

"Okay. If you say so." But he grinned as if he knew exactly what was going on.

Amy pushed back from the table and gathered up their plates, needing to be doing something to distract her mind.

"Would you like a refill on the iced tea?"

"I can get it. First, I want to take a turn around the property. I know you've got a top-of-the-line security setup. Grillo walked me through it, but I want to take time checking everything for myself. Then I want to ask you some questions about the neighborhood."

She paused with her hands full of dishes. "The neighborhood? Why? Dan and Security Solutions checked out everything down to the last stop sign before I bought the house and moved in."

"I want to do some studying of my own," he told her. "It helps to know who the neighbors are, when and if they have company, who walks their dogs. Stuff like that. It's easier to spot anomalies that way."

The dishes rattled as her hands started to shake, so she set them back down on the table.

"Anomalies?"

"You know. When people have company. And have parties. That kind of stuff. Just anything not part of daily life."

She had to swallow twice before she could speak. "You think he could come here? Quinn, he's in prison."

"Yes, he is, and he's put you in a virtual one." He took a step forward and cupped her face in his warm, strong hands. "A prison I'm going to help you break out of. Okay?"

She nodded, hoping he was right but afraid he might not be.

"Amy, we may have just met in person today, but we've been talking to each other for a long time. Trust me when I tell you, one of the reasons I took this job was because I wanted to see if we could have something together." He studied her with those ebony eyes. "I hope that doesn't frighten you."

She actually managed a smile. "There are a lot of things that frighten me, Quinn, but that's not one of them. For years I haven't trusted anyone except Dan and the security agents, but I trusted you from the beginning. More than them. I never believed in serendipity until Tex connected us, although I guess it really began when Tex decided to answer my questions."

"For which I'll always be grateful to him."

For a moment, Amy thought he was going to kiss her, and she held her breath, wondering how she'd react. Then he dropped his hands.

"The agency gave me a schematic of the security system, and Grillo gave me all the codes. But what happens if there's a power failure?"

"We thought of that. There are battery-powered sensors on all the windows, hidden by the shutters. If someone kills the main system, those sensors send a signal to base and someone heads out here right away."

"Okay. Let me do my recon outside now. Then I'll be ready for some more iced tea."

The kitchen window looked out on the side yard. Amy usually kept the lower half of the shutters closed so no one could see directly into the house. Which was stupid, she always told herself, since no one could get onto her property. But today she tilted them open enough so she could watch Quinn on his rounds. Even his search was done with an economy of movement, as he carefully separated branches and bushes and checked the eaves of the buildings. She knew he'd remember the exact placement of each camera.

It was fascinating to watch him. She could almost

imagine him on a covert mission, stealthy. Careful, focused. Dedicated. She felt weird moving from window to window so she could keep watching him, but he fascinated her. And she wanted to see how thorough a job he did.

She had just lost sight of him at the corner of the house when a loud rapping made her jump nearly out of her skin. She was glad she wasn't holding anything or she was sure she'd have dropped it. She looked toward the sound and saw Quinn standing at the sliding glass doors to the patio, looking in on her and rapping gently on the glass.

She went to the doors and slid them apart just enough so he could slip inside.

"I didn't want to just walk in and scare the bejeesus out of you." His mouth curved in the grin she was becoming addicted to. "Although I did see you spying on me."

Heat crept up her cheeks for the second time that day. "I wasn't spying. Just making sure you were okay."

He laughed, a hearty, natural sound she felt all the way to her toes.

"If you say so. How about some of that iced tea and we can sit and chat."

She nodded. "Okay. You can ask me anything you want to."

"Anything?"

Amy swallowed a sigh. She was used to people

asking her questions, but with Quinn she had a feeling somehow it would be easier.

"Yes." She looked directly at him. "I said it before. I trust you."

He was standing directly in front of her now and, for a wild moment, she wondered again if he was going to kiss her. She hadn't been kissed in so long—hadn't *wanted* to be kissed—that she wasn't sure she'd know what to do if he did. Push him away? Throw her arms around him? Run out of the room?

He cupped her face in his warm palms as he had earlier, and his touch sent an unfamiliar feeling of warmth and security rushing through her. What would it be like, she wondered, to just let herself go after all this time? To feel a man's arms around her, the touch of his lips on hers, the—

"Amy?" Quinn's voice broke through her thoughts. "You okay?" He was staring directly into her eyes, studying her.

She wet her lips. "Uh, yes. I'm good. Thanks."

Except she could hardly breathe.

He smiled, and again she felt it through her entire body.

"Good. Let's go hang out in those comfortable-looking chairs you've got, and I can tell you what I learned about agoraphobia, and you can tell me all about Matt the Asshat."

Amy laughed, something she'd hardly done for the past ten years.

"I love that. It makes him seem…less formidable."

"Good. Then that's what we'll call him."

When he stepped away to allow her to refill their glasses, she felt an unfamiliar emptiness, as if she'd lost something. Oh god. She was in big trouble here, but the kind of trouble she hadn't even been close to in years.

* * *

Matthew had convinced Jamie that flying to Florida would result in too many problems. They'd need identification to check in at the airline and to board the plane. Jamie had used plenty of money to procure flawless identification for them, but what if his picture was already being circulated? He kept checking the television in the hotel and then on the iPhone Jamie had purchased for him and nothing had showed up. He had a feeling they were keeping this quiet, mostly for the sake of his prissy stepsister, but that didn't mean his picture wasn't being circulated to other agencies.

That was another reason he'd insisted on the purchase of a car. He wanted control over his own transportation, even if it meant long hours on the road. Every time they rented a car, one of them would have to show a driver's license. No one knew about Jamie and their relationship, but he didn't trust the federal agencies that could dig up anything. No, they'd be better off always having control of their transportation.

He'd volunteered to do most of the driving to Tampa. He was so wired he knew he wouldn't sleep anyway, and Jamie, who hated long-distance driving, was grateful for the offer. They started out that night when they knew there'd be less traffic on the road. The trip took a little less than twenty-four hours.

One time when they stopped to eat, he scoured the Internet for pictures of people who lived in south Tampa and what they wore. The answer was…everything. Everything from tailored slacks and hand-sewn dress shirts to khakis and T-shirts.

They made a stop in Ocala, north of Tampa, where Matthew did some shopping for specific clothes and a decent enough wig that, unless someone got close up to him, looked natural. He settled on slacks and a sport shirt as the perfect outfit for his reconnaissance trip. He'd leave the moustache when he shaved, just as he planned. It would alter the whole appearance of his face. Sometimes people fixated on something like that and never remembered the actual face.

He changed in the restroom of a gas station where he could put on the wig, too. He figured it would be best to establish the image ahead of time so if he was spotted, again, they'd only have the description he wanted them to have.

"Not bad." Jamie looked at him with a grin. "Not bad at all."

They arrived in Tampa late at night, and Jamie had been willing to settle for the first chain motel they came to but not Matthew. He wanted a fancy hotel with all the luxuries, including twenty-four-hour room service. Again, ten years of deprivation had left him with an obsessive need for the good life.

"Let's compromise," Jamie suggested. "Someplace rich but not high profile. It's less than three days since we broke you out. You have no idea how many agencies are looking for you, but you can bet they'll figure you'll come to Tampa right away to finish what you started that night."

"Okay, but not one of those chain hotels again. I want a soft bed and rich food."

Jamie did a quick search on the Internet and found a hotel in the Hyde Park area that fit the bill. Top quality, considered elite, but not the kind of place where people would be searching for them. It did not have the visibility of the luxury hotels downtown on the waterfront.

"Perfect," Matthew told him, luxuriating in the softness of the bed and the expensive little touches in the room.

Now, after a room service breakfast with gourmet foods, he was ready to scout the area where Miss Priss lived. See what the best way was to get to her. He wanted a good length of time with her when he did so he could take out all the frustrations of the past ten years. Make that the past twenty. Oh yeah. He could hardly wait.

Jamie took the wheel this time, having been here before and practically memorized the entire area. That was one of Jamie's many talents, an eidetic memory that retained encyclopedias of information. They drove out of the downtown area, taking scenic Bayshore Boulevard that ran along the waterfront before curving deep into the historic South Tampa area. Mature trees and lush vegetation created a rich environment that accented the streets lined with predominantly Spanish architecture that spoke of the city's history.

Maybe he'd buy a place for himself here, after everything was taken care of. On the waterfront, with a big cabin cruiser he could take out into the Bay. Tampa was a good place to keep his business going, too. Jamie had followed instructions to the letter and kept it growing at an amazing rate while Matthew was in prison. Yes, life was indeed going to be good for him.

Finally.

They turned onto yet another street lined with massive Spanish-style homes. He spotted two different people walking dogs, and a little auto traffic, but mostly there was little activity. This was not like a suburban neighborhood, where people hung out on the streets and kids played in the front yards. That meant they needed to be extra careful not to attract any undue attention.

"We're coming up on it in the next block," Jamie

told him. "It's on this side of the street. Fourth house on the right. You can't miss the iron fencing."

And there it was, the little bitch's fortress, just as described.

"She never leaves the house," Jamie reminded him. "Landscapers and housekeepers are from bonded services. She never sits in the yard. And I told you about her deliveries. Man. You really frightened the shit out of her."

Matthew laughed, his first real laugh in a long time. "Good. That makes me feel better."

As they drove slowly past the house, Matthew lifted his camera to the windshield and snapped picture after picture as fast as he could. At the corner, Jamie turned and headed down the side street.

"I spent a little time on this street on each visit," Jamie told him. "Rented different cars each time. People are sensitive to anything out of the norm here, and I sure didn't want to call attention to myself."

"Smart," Matthew agreed. "Can we do once more around the block?"

"Just once," Jamie agreed. "That's it. I mean it. I don't want to tempt fate."

"Fine. I just want to fix it all in my mind and take some pictures. The only way in is over that fence. When you figure out how to breach it, I want the layout fixed in my mind."

"Fine. But just once more."

Jamie drove through the entire neighborhood

before rerunning to Amy's street. He only slowed a hair as they began to pass the house.

"Damn." Mathew blew out a breath. "I thought I saw someone in her yard, just a brief glimpse, but there's no one there now."

"She does have people there occasionally. I told you that. Landscapers, housekeepers, security agents. Did you see any lawn equipment?"

"No." Matthew nearly growled his answer. "Besides, didn't you say they always wore suits?"

"Yes but not the workers. Anyway, the agent could have worn something different today. And, if there are no yard work people, he wouldn't stay long. Just until he completed whatever errand sent him there. Matthew, I'm telling you, no stranger is going to suddenly show up. I've studied that house and her routine for months."

"And by the way, exactly how did you do that?"

Jamie laughed. "There are so many ways to scope out a neighborhood over time, things people don't even think about. Trust me. I did it, and I didn't raise any eyebrows. And there's no new man in her life."

"I'm just being thorough, like you told me you were."

"Glad to hear you say that because I'd hate to have gone to all this trouble to get your ass free only to have them grab you up again right away."

"Yeah, me, either. Okay, let's get going."

He knew they wouldn't have much time to put his

plan into action. As soon as the warden knew he was gone, the US Marshals would be called, as well as that fucking attorney, and a full-out manhunt would be in place. That was fine. He could move swiftly. He needed to get into the house, grab the bitch, get her out of there, and hide her until he was finished with her.

God! This was almost as good as sex.

* * *

Quinn took another turn around the property, making sure the camera lenses were clear and nobody at the houses on either side was trying to get a glimpse of the housebound neighbor. Security Solutions had provided him with a thorough analysis of the neighborhood, part of a report they'd prepared for Rendell when he was looking for places to relocate Amy. He knew all the residents were wealthy, in varying degrees. Many were part of Tampa society. There were attorneys, bankers, investment counselors, politicians, real estate moguls. Dan Rendell had also made him aware of the hefty inheritance Amy had received, which allowed for the original purchase of the house, as well as the tidy sums she received from her video games.

He knew the neighbors minded their own business, did not socialize unless they ran into each other while walking their dogs. And they mostly minded their own business, which was probably why Dan—and Amy—had chosen this area. Good. He didn't want nosy people poking into her business, especially after today's phone call, which he replayed in his mind.

"Better prepare yourself for a shocker," Rendell said the moment he answered Quinn's call.

"Lay it on me."

"Matthew Baker escaped from prison."

Years of SEAL training had prevented him for showing the intense shock he felt at the news, but he was well and truly stunned. How could a mass murderer just escape? Weren't they kept in a special kind of cell? Watched constantly?

"What the fuck?" Then he caught himself. "Excuse me, sir, I—"

"No apology necessary. I almost said as much myself. It seems one of the guards, an eight-year veteran, thought a hefty amount of money was worth more than doing his job. I suppose I can't blame him. The guards don't make huge sums of money."

"But they're supposed to have integrity," Quinn protested. "They—"

"Yes," Rendell broke in. "But human nature is what it is. The Marshals have mounted a national manhunt and tapped into every agency possible. We're sitting on releasing it to the media because I do not want Amy to find out. She's enough of a basket case as it is."

"I get it."

"We don't know if he's aware she's still alive, but if he somehow discovered it, she's in very grave danger."

"Sir. I trained for things like this for fifteen years. I

assure you she's safe with me. I won't let her out of my sight."

"I knew we made the right choice with you." Rendell paused. "I don't want to ask Security Solutions to send more guys out to help you. That's like waving a red flag. But Baker is very devious, and, despite your training and skills, if he breaches the security, one man might not be enough to stop him."

"I'd like to disagree with you, but you don't know me well enough to accept the fact I can handle this. However, I've got an idea. Let me make some calls, and I'll get back to you. Meanwhile, vigilant is the word."

"Keep in touch," Rendell insisted. "And keep your eye on her at all times."

"Count on it."

Now, as he walked at a leisurely pace, admiring all the landscaping, he turned some ideas over in his mind. When he had them firmed up, first he'd call Tex and get his input. Then he'd suggest it to Amy without telling her the reason for it. He'd just have to take a couple of days guiding her in that direction.

Decision made, he headed back into the house to deal with another problem. More than one. For one thing, he wasn't comfortable sleeping in the guest cottage and leaving Amy alone by herself in the house. On the other hand, the more time he spent in close proximity to her, the harder it was to keep reminding himself that she was dealing with a severe psychological problem and sex wasn't even on her to-do list.

He'd just have to take himself in hand until he could develop their relationship more. And that's what it was to him. A relationship, no matter how he looked at it. What started out as an effort to get Tex off his back by socializing online with her had created feelings he'd never expected. And today, when he'd finally met her in person, all the things he'd heard about, all the things Tex had told him about when you meet *the one* dropped right into their slots.

They had a long way to go, however, between Baker, Amy's nightmares, and her agoraphobia. And this was the worst possible time to try coaxing her out of the house. Maybe he could get her onto the patio. He couldn't believe that for the first nine years she lived here, she'd never even opened the sliding door to get a breath of fresh air. But the patio was safe, not visible from the street, and he'd be sure to keep his trusty Glock 9mm tucked in the waistband of his jeans at all times, along with the knife he'd wear strapped to his calf.

Okay, then. First order of business—talk to Amy about the sleeping arrangements. And keep himself from telling her she'd be much safer if they were in the same bed.

CHAPTER 9

"Quinn? Oh god. Quinn. Come here. Please."

Amy had just finished loading the dishwasher, thinking how odd yet comforting it was to have more than two dishes to clean. Even odder to remember that Quinn had only been here for less than a day, yet she felt as if he'd been here forever.

She glanced at the laptop sitting on the counter, out of habit, stunned when its screen suddenly went blank.

"What?" He moved as fast as his leg allowed. "What's the matter?"

She pointed at the screen. "The security system is out."

"Impossible. You've got too many safeguards, in addition to the battery-operated sensors on the windows."

"But they aren't foolproof," she protested. "We need to call the agency."

As Quinn pulled his cell from his pants pocket, it rang in his hand.

"Molloy." He listened. "Yeah. Uh-huh. Uh-huh. Uh-huh. Okay, we'll watch for it and call you back."

"What is it?" Her heart was thumping so hard it hurt her chest. "What's wrong?"

"That was the agency. The alarm sounded there as soon as your system went down so they began checking it at once. Seems some thieves have been targeting this neighborhood for robberies, using an RF jammer to disrupt security systems."

"God." Her hand went to her throat. "Are they out there now?"

"Yes but not for long. Hold on. Okay, look." He pointed at the laptop. "Your system's back up. The guy at Security Solutions said they'd been told the police were on it and, in fact, had an unmarked car stashed in a driveway. Seems these have been occurring like clockwork every so many nights."

"Did they catch them yet?"

"I think—Hold on." His phone had rung again, so he pushed the Accept button. "Molloy. Yeah? Uh-huh. Uh-huh." He listened for a moment. "Great. Thanks for the update." He ended the call and put his hands on Amy's shoulders, looking directly at her. "They got them. It wasn't hard after all. Seems one of the thieves is the son of one of the homeowners. They've been targeting homes when they know someone is out for the night, information which apparently is easy for them to get.

They actually made a mistake with yours. They were trying to hit the house next door."

Her body went so limp with relief he had to put his arms around her to hold her upright. He stroked her hair, his touch so soothing she didn't ever want him to stop.

"It's okay. They weren't after you. It has nothing to do with Matthew."

"I know." She sighed against his chest. "I have to keep telling myself he's locked up tight as a drum and can't get to me, but that fear is always there."

"Nobody will get to you now that I'm here. Count on it." He put his hand beneath her chin and lifted her face. "Why don't you have a cup of tea and come watch some television. Take your mind off it."

"That's okay. The tea sounds great, but I think I'm going to work on the video game for a while."

"Sounds good to me." Quinn nodded. "Okay with you if I hang out in your family room and watch television for a while?"

"Um, sure." Amy bit her lower lip. "I guess. I'm just not used to—"

"I know," he broke in, and grinned. "Strangers in the house. But we made it through the afternoon okay, and I'm hoping we aren't anymore. Strangers, that is."

"Of course."

She'd learned more about her condition from him that afternoon than she had in ten years with Dr. Ybarra. And she loved listening to him. His voice had a slight rough quality to it, but it was also warm and surrounded her like a security blanket. Even Patience had given him her stamp of approval. After sniffing him several times and brushing against his legs, she had actually jumped into his lap, curled around herself, and begun to purr. And Amy trusted the cat's intuition even more than that of a human.

It was so odd how at ease he made her feel. She hadn't been sure that nearly a month of online conversation would translate to anything in person, so she was amazed that it had. And not only did she not want him to leave and go out to the guest cottage, she liked the feeling she had with him in the house. Safe. Secure.

Special.

Don't get ahead of yourself, kiddo. He might see things differently, and you have no idea how to behave with a man anymore.

"Go on and do your thing," he told her, picking up the television remote. "I'll flip through your gazillion channels and find something to watch."

"Okay. Help yourself to anything. You know, like a cold drink or something."

"Thanks."

She fixed her tea, wondering for a moment if there was any special reason he was staying in the house. And it occurred to her that she hadn't once had the urge to shut herself away from him in her room. She realized they'd been okay together all day, and he might not want to be alone yet. She treated herself to one last look at him stretched out in one of the big lounge chairs, remote in hand, before heading to the room she'd set up as her workroom.

As she woke up her computers and logged in to begin working, she thought back to their conversation after lunch. He told her what he'd learned about agoraphobia, impressing her with the extent of his research. He also told her that it was possible to get past it in very small stages. Dr. Ybarra had been telling her the same thing, but also pointing out that it was better if she had someone help her that she trusted completely.

Was Quinn that person? She certainly, unexpectedly, felt safer and more comfortable with him than any other of the few people in her life. That included the security agents and even Dan Rendell, who had been her lifeline for ten years.

She tried to work on the next level of the SEAL game, but her brain would not focus. All she could think about was Quinn, his hard body relaxing in her family room. The slightly raspy sound of his voice. Her unexpected reaction at seeing him in person. For the first time, she wasn't counting the minutes until whoever was inside her house left.

Finally, unable to make herself concentrate on her work, she shut everything down and walked back into the family room. Quinn was just as she'd left him, and the sight did strange things to her body. Unfamiliar things. Although she moved quietly, he put the television on pause as soon as she entered the room, and looked at her, a question on his face.

"Having trouble with the game?" he guessed.

She shrugged. "Guess I'm just not in the mood to work tonight."

You don't need to leave the house to have sex, a tiny voice whispered.

Good lord. She really needed to get hold of herself. Ten years in isolation, and suddenly she felt like a horny teenager. She hadn't even known she remembered what that was like.

"Come watch television with me for a while. Maybe that will relax your brain."

She wished something would. She was tempted to accept his invitation, but she thought she should get to the safety of her bedroom before she did something that embarrassed her. And him. She couldn't believe what was happening to her after ten years of physical and emotional isolation.

She needed to get away from him for a while and gather her wits about her.

"Thanks, but I've been up since before six this morning. I think I'll get some sleep." She paused, wet her lips. "Are you going out to the cottage now?"

He looked at her as if he could see everything inside her head, but that damn smile eased everything.

"I thought I'd hang here for a while, if it's okay with you.

"Sure. No problem. See you in the morning.

"Why don't you have breakfast with me?" The words were out of her mouth before she realized it. "If you don't want to, that's okay. I mean—"

"I'd love to. Thanks." He rose from the chair and walked to where she was standing. "Here's the thing, Amy. I want you to be comfortable. My job is to make you feel safe. If you don't want me in here, just tell me. I'll take my cue from you."

"Have breakfast with me." The words practically fell out of her mouth.

"I get up very early."

"So do I," she told him. "See you in the morning."

She made it to her bedroom and fell onto the bed, wondering who the hell was taking over her mind and body. She forced herself to lie there while she pulled her scattered thoughts together, reminding herself not to read things into Quinn's words and actions. She was sure he was just being kind to a nutjob, no matter what he said.

She went through her nightly routine, donning her gown, washing her face, brushing her teeth. She adjusted the shutters so that while the view was still blocked, she allowed moonlight in. She lay back on her pillows and did the deep breathing exercises that Dr. Ybarra had taught her and, after a while, she drifted off into a dream.

"You're so beautiful." Quinn's rough voice caressed her. "I want to kiss your body everywhere."

His words sent shivers along her spine.

"Yes." She whispered the word. "Do that. Please."

Her gown had disappeared at some point, and she lay naked beneath him, body throbbing with need. He gave her lips a gentle lick, the touch like a rough caress, before pressing the tip so she would open and allow his tongue inside. She slid her own over his, reveling in the taste. When he sucked hard to pull her own tongue into his mouth, heat raced everywhere in her body and, between her legs, her sex throbbed with unfamiliar need.

When he lifted his head and broke the contact, she wanted to cry, but then he drew a line of soft kisses along her jaw and down her neck. Every nerve in her body vibrated, and that need inside her grew. Even as he continued to move his mouth over her skin, she pressed herself against him, feeling the swollen length of his cock. She wanted to feel that hardness inside her, filling her, driving into her.

"Quinn." She whispered the word. "God, Quinn."

"No." His laugh was guttural. "Not God. Just me."

With that, he moved his head down so he could capture a nipple between his teeth. He bit down lightly and tugged on it, sent hot fire through her. He worked it for a long time before shifting to the other one and giving it the same treatment. Her body was screaming with need, and her sex was aching and hungry.

He finally released the second nipple with a soft pop! He slid down her body, stringing kisses everywhere, pausing to lick her navel and run his tongue around the furled flesh. And then he was between her thighs, his broad shoulders holding them open, his thumbs pressing apart the lips of her sex.

"God, Amy. Just…god."

He blew on the hot flesh, sending her need rising even more. But then he traced the length of her slit with his tongue, pausing to give special attention to her clit, and she nearly screamed with the pleasure.

"More," she demanded. "Please. More."

But he wasn't going to rush this. He took his time, stroking her clit with his tongue, tugging on it with his teeth before finally sliding one finger into her hot, waiting flesh. She clamped down on it, but it wasn't nearly enough.

"More," she begged again. "Don't stop."

He added a second finger, scissoring them to stretch her because she was so tight, before sliding in a third.

"Get ready, baby," he growled.

Clamping his lips around her clit, he fucked her with his fingers, in and out, harder and faster, one arm around her body holding her in place. She'd been starved for this for so long that it seemed just seconds before she exploded and the climax roared through her. He tightened the grip with his arm to steady her while, with his fingers, he drove her through the release.

At last the spasms subsided, and he eased his fingers

from her body, pausing to take one more suck of her hot bud of a clit.

"Quinn," she moaned.

That had been wonderful, more than she'd had in forever, but she didn't want to stop now. She wanted to feel him inside her. Feel the walls of her sex clutch around him while he fucked her brains out.

"Patience, baby," he murmured in that raspy voice of his. "I thought that would take the edge off enough to give you a little patience."

"I don't have patience where you're concerned. I've waited too long for this."

And that was the damn truth, she told herself.

"Give me a second here."

He shifted and, when she opened her eyes, she saw him reaching for the condom he'd placed on her nightstand. When he raised up on his knees to roll it on, she couldn't help staring at the thick, swollen length of his cock and wondering if it would all fit inside her. It had been so very long, and she just hoped the orgasm she'd already had would make it easier for her body to accept him.

She watched as he sheathed himself then spread her legs wide again.

"We'll take it slow," he promised, "at least as slow as I can. Fuck, Amy, you can't believe how bad I want you."

She planted her feet on either side of him, knees

bent to facilitate him, and held her breath as the tip of his cock touched her opening.

"Deep breath, Amy. Come on. That's it," he encouraged when she did as he instructed.

Slowly, slowly, he eased himself inside her, stretching her walls until she was sure there was no more room. And still he moved farther, deeper. By the time she'd taken all of him, she felt as if every space in her body was filled.

Quinn leaned forward and took her mouth in a hungry kiss, sucking on her tongue while his hands cupped her breasts and his fingers teased and pinched her nipples. She was more aroused than she'd ever been in her life, although those memories were of a much younger Amy. Every inch of her body wanted him—his tongue, his lips, his hands, his cock.

"Jesus!" he groaned. "This is better than anything I imagined. God, Amy." He drew in a breath and let it out. "Okay, deep breath, sugar. We're going for a hard ride."

And that's exactly what it was. At first, he eased himself in and out, a little at a time, more each time he entered her again. Then he increased his pace, driving harder, faster. He slid his hands beneath her butt, and she wrapped her legs around his waist, lifting herself to him and clasping his body tighter to hers. On and on it went, until her mind was a blank and there was nothing but the two of them on this hard ride.

"Getting close," he gritted.

He moved one hand to slide his fingers over her clit, rubbing it hard and fast.

And that was all it took.

They came together, his engorged cock pulsing inside her, the walls of her sex spasming around him, the two of them moving in perfect sync.

And then, when she was sure she had no breath left, the spasms began to subside. Quinn leaned forward and wrapped his arms around her, placing a soft kiss on her lips. He held her through all the aftershocks, murmuring sweet things in her ear.

She had no idea how long they lay there together, thundering heartbeats slowing, breaths easing, her body too weak to move.

"Stay right here," he told her. "I'll be right back."

He eased out of her body and off her bed, heading for the bathroom to dispose of the condom. His absence left her feeling suddenly bereft and she cried out.

"No. No, don't do that. No."

The sound of her own voice woke her out of her dream, and she sat up in bed, shocked to find her hand between her thighs and her heart pounding. At that exact moment, the door to her room slammed open, and Quinn appeared. Gun in hand, looking left to right.

"I've got it," he assured her. "Don't move. Did someone get into this fortress?"

The heat of embarrassment flooded her face. How

exactly did she explain this? Then he saw the covers tossed back, her nightgown rucked up and her hand between her legs, and froze in place.

Holy god, now what did she do?

"I heard you cry out," he told her as he stuck the gun back into the waistband of his jeans. I didn't think anyone could get in but hell, Amy, you scared the shit out of me." His gaze landed again on where her hand was, and she realized it was still between her legs. She yanked it back and pulled up the covers.

"I'm fine," she croaked. "Sorry to disturb you. You can go back to your television. And, by the way, forget what you saw here."

His mouth curved in the grin she loved so much. "That's kind of hard, darlin'. I think it's burned into my brain."

"Quinn…"

"I think maybe this is something we should talk about, but I'll leave if you really want me to."

She looked down at her lap. "I'm so embarrassed."

"Nothing to be embarrassed about. I do it myself sometimes."

Her eyes widened. "You do?"

"Uh-huh. Actually, a lot more since we started talking online."

He had been slowly moving toward her bed until he stopped right beside it. He eased the gun from where he'd stashed it and placed it on the nightstand.

Amy stared at it.

"Just in case, although I don't expect to need it. Not with all your security. I still feel safer with it though."

Without even being aware he was doing it, she found him sitting on the bed beside her now, one leg beside hers, the bad one, the other on the floor. And, somehow, his arm was now around her, holding her gently against his very hot, very hard body.

"You okay?" he asked in his rough but warm voice.

"Um, yes. I think so."

She was stunned to realize that was the truth. She, who had hardly been able to speak to the few people who did work for her for the past ten years, was sitting in her bed with a man she'd just met today. No, not just today, she reminded herself. A few weeks ago. And that instant connection had come out of nowhere.

"No nightmares tonight," she told him in a stunned voice.

"Yeah? Maybe I should have been doing it to chase away mine."

"You have nightmares, too?"

He nodded. "I'll tell you mine if you tell me yours."

"Uh, okay."

"Then," he said in a low, sexy tone, "how about telling me about your dream? Maybe we can make it come true."

Matthew sat on the balcony of their hotel suite, sipping

Pappy van Winkle bourbon in a glass with two ice cubes. Just two. Otherwise, it diluted what had to be the smoothest bourbon in the world. It felt good to be sitting in the tropical environment with the sun on his face and a soft breeze keeping the temperature comfortable. He had wanted to stay in Tampa, but Jamie had convinced him of the wisdom of hauling ass out of there.

"Just for a couple of days, until I can make sure they don't have an army there hunting for you. You know they'll expect you to head right for her."

Matthew snorted. "They'd be right."

"Which is why we're leaving instead of staying."

They had been here for only twenty-four hours, yet, to him, it felt like a week. The boutique hotel on the Gulf of Mexico was a great place to hang out after ten years in that fucking cell. The gourmet food, the massages, the outdoor spa were all wonderful and had eased the fidgets for a while, but he was done. He wanted to take care of his main reason for breaking out. Then he could collect the rest of his money, and he and Jamie could move to some tropical island that did not have an extradition treaty with the United States.

He'd been haunting the Internet for any word of his escape, alternating between feeling furious that the fucking attorney Rendell apparently had that kind of clout and the need to focus on his objective. Killing fucking Miss Priss. He was done waiting. He would convince Jamie to do one more analysis of the situation, and then he would finish putting his plan together. And get it done.

He was letting a taste of it roll around on his tongue when Jamie walked out onto the balcony and dropped into the other chair.

"It's nice to see you relaxing like this. I hope you can handle it for a while because now is not the time to jump."

Matthew glanced over at his companion. "How long is a while?" He swallowed some bourbon. "Exactly."

"I don't know yet." Jamie looked over and grinned. "Exactly."

Matthew tossed down the rest of the bourbon. "What the fuck is going on, Jamie?"

"Like you keep saying, money can buy anything, including information. Your Miss Priss has a man living with her now. A guy who looks like he'd rip your head off before breakfast."

Matthew sat up with an abrupt movement. "What the fuck? What man? Who is he? What the hell is he doing there? Jesus! I thought you said she didn't have any friends, especially male friends."

"I'm trying to find out more about him but, as you are well aware, learning anything that has to do with her is harder than digging for gold."

Matthew stared at him for a long time. "Tell me, Jamie, how did you manage to get all the information you've gotten so far? And who are you in contact with about this guy in Miss Priss's yard?"

Jamie looked at him, smirking. "I told you, all it takes is money. Plus, I had all that time on my hands while you were locked up. I did some traveling. Made some contacts, which I chose carefully, by the way."

"I hope to fuck you mean that."

Jamie looked at him, frowning. "Have I ever lied to you? Was I the one who made your life miserable? Pissed all over you like all those others? No. I was not. You told me I'm all you have and all you want. That you trust me. Matt, I'd do anything for you. Please believe me that I'm not being stupid about any of this."

Matthew smiled. Of course he could trust Jamie. And no one else.

"Sorry about that. I'm just suspicious of everyone."

"With good reason," Jamie agreed. "But not me."

"No. Not you. Okay, go on and do what you have to. Get that guy checked out. Plug into whatever sources you have and see if there's a big manhunt out for me in Tampa because I want to leave here in no more than two days."

"Two days?" Jamie stared at him.

"I've thought about her for ten years," he said. "I kept seeing that image of her again, over and over, her arm moving, her head lifting. Not sure if she was dead or alive but my gut telling me she had survived. And waiting all this time for the chance to finish her off. And you know why."

Jamie smirked. "I do. That's one of the reasons I

want you to be careful. I don't want anything to happen to you."

"Me, either. So get busy and do your thing."

He followed Jamie into the room so he could refill his drink then stood looking out as he sipped his bourbon. He was already imagining all the things he would do to that prissy little bitch.

CHAPTER 10

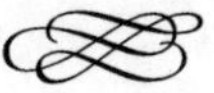

Quinn opened his eyes and had to think for a moment to remember where he was. Oh yeah. Still in his jeans and T-shirt. In Amy's bed. With Amy. Who was in what he could only call a dowager nightgown, under the covers but nestled tight against his shoulder. Patience was curled up at the foot of the bed, staring at them with unblinking eyes. He wondered how he'd feel having sex with the cat watching them.

Don't get too far ahead of yourself, guy. One step at a time. First, make sure last night doesn't turn into a horror show for her.

His arm was still around her, and, from its stiffness, he figured it had been that way all night. Taking great care, he eased it out from beneath her body, but even so, she stirred and half-opened her eyes.

"Quinn."

He gave a low laugh. “It better be. I’d have to kill someone else if I found them in bed with you.”

Her eyes popped wide open, and she sat up, a pretty blush painting her cheeks.

“Oh lord. Did I—Did we—”

He tilted up her face and pressed a soft kiss to her lips. “No, but after you told me about your dream, I had a hard time keeping myself from it.”

“I told you about my dream?” A blush climbed up her face. “I told you about my dream.”

He grinned. “You sure did. Reluctantly at first, I have to add, but then I managed to coax every detail out of you.”

She buried her face in his shoulder. “I can’t believe I did that. Any of it.”

He reclined against the pillow and pulled her over so she lay on his body, her face close to his.

“Let me tell you something, darlin’. Having sex with you vicariously was ten times better than having real sex with most of the women I’ve known. And, I’m ashamed to say, that number is quite high.”

She stared at him. “You’re not lying to me?”

“I’d never lie to you, Amy. Ever. Count on it.” He cruised his mouth over hers.

“Ugh.” She made a face. “I haven’t brushed my teeth yet.”

“Me, either. And I definitely need a shower.”

“Me, too.”

He winked. "Maybe we could shower together."

"Shower? Together?" she squeaked, and he saw a faint blush creep up her cheeks.

Quinn chuckled. "I love watching you blush. And yes, together. But maybe we'll save that for tonight. For now, I'll be satisfied with a kiss." He groaned. "Any more than that, and I'll be in big trouble."

His swollen cock pressed against his fly, and he was sure she could feel it even through the two layers of clothing. When she wriggled against him, and her lips turned up in a grin, he knew he was right.

"Better be careful," he warned. "A man can only take so much."

The grin disappeared, replaced by a serious expression.

"I—" She stopped and turned her head to the side. "I've never done what I did last night. Either thing, especially telling a man about it. In fact, you should know that the last time I had sex was ten years ago, and it wasn't a lot to write home about."

He cupped her chin and tilted her face up to his. "I promise you that's going to change."

"This whole thing has hit me like a lightning storm, but you know something? And, Quinn, this is so totally weird and out of character for me. I feel as if I've known you forever. And I trust you. I felt that way right from our first online conversation."

"Me, too." He kissed her again. "I finally believe in

fate, darlin'. So on that note, how about if we get up and start our day. I have to exercise my leg, and I want to do some more research on your stepbrother and his family before his father married your mother."

"Why?" she interrupted.

"Because he has to have someone helping him. Security Solutions and Dan Rendell may have checked things out, but I don't know if they went back before Harrison married your mother."

"I know his first wife died," she told him. "He and Mom were both widowed, which was sort of what brought them together. But no one ever discussed his first wife. As far as Matthew himself is concerned, nothing turned up. No friends. No women. Nothing."

"No sweat. I have contacts they don't, so I'm going to put them to good use."

Amy placed a soft kiss on his lips. "Thank you."

"No problem. And I suggest you get your coding work done during the daylight hours because I've got plans for tonight."

"Oh you do?" She grinned and a tiny, tiny dimple flashed at the left corner of her mouth. Then she sobered. "Go slow with me, Quinn. I don't even know if I'm any good at this."

"Darlin', we'll go as slow as you want. I'm heading for the cottage to work out and shower. How about breakfast together?"

"That sounds good."

But she stayed in the same position, and he could tell she was running something through her mind.

"What is it, Amy? Spit it out."

She kept her eyes lowered when she said, "Would it be okay if—if I asked you to move your stuff into the house?"

He wanted to pump his fist, but he restrained himself.

"Yes, it would be fine. In fact, a great idea. But, Amy? I'm going to move into one of the guest rooms. I'll be in this room as long as you want, but I want you to have some space if you need it. I wasn't even sure you'd furnished them, as a matter of fact."

"Dan Rendell insisted I get furniture for them when I moved in, I guess hoping one day I'd invite people to visit. You're the first one besides me to sleep here in ten years."

He smiled. "And it's my pleasure. Like I said, I just want to be sure you don't feel crowded or pressured for anything."

She grinned up at him. "Is it any wonder I feel the way I do about you?"

He didn't want to ask her what that was. Too soon. Instead, he gave her ass a light smack. "Now, let's get our day started."

He was actually whistling when he headed out the sliding doors and jogged to the cottage. His good mood lasted until he was in the living room and the cell phone in his jeans sounded its ringtone. When he looked at the screen, he saw Dan Rendell's name.

Uh-oh. This could only mean trouble.

He tapped to answer. "Molloy."

"Molloy, it's Dan Rendell."

"I know. Your name came up on the screen. What's up? I have a feeling it can't be good."

"Bad hardly describes it." He cleared his throat. "I just had a call from the cemetery where Amy's family is buried, and where she is, too, supposedly."

"And?" he prompted.

"I had ordered flowers for the graves. Today would have been Marilyn Baker's birthday, and I felt the need to do something, in light of recent circumstances."

"Go on." Was he going to drag this out?

"The caretaker just called me. He says it looks like someone dug up Amy's grave."

Quinn's stomach knotted, and nausea surged in his mouth. Holy shit. "Exactly how could he tell? I'm sure whoever it was didn't leave it open for everyone to see."

"You're right. In fact," he said, "whoever it was did such a good job if he hadn't been doing some maintenance before placing the flowers, he'd never have noticed it. And, Quinn?"

"Yeah?" His hand tightened on the phone.

"He said he checked, and the casket was opened, too. There were some scratches on the mahogany around the locks."

Shit, fuck, and damn.

"They know she's alive." It was a statement, not a question.

"That doubles the danger she's in."

Quinn wanted to tell the man he figured that out for himself, but he swallowed his words. "No one will get to her, I promise you that." Damn straight. "Do you have any idea who could be helping Baker? Because this was obviously done before his escape."

"Not a clue. I didn't know Harrison before he and Marilyn were married. I was a friend of her late husband's. That's how I knew her and then him."

"Don't you think we'd better look into his life before that?"

"Already on it." His words were edged with controlled anger. "And I'm kicking myself for not doing it before, but Harrison's first wife wasn't even on my radar. A lesson I'll remember in the future."

Quinn really wanted to throttle the man and ask him why no one had thought of this before.

"Keep me in the loop. And by the way, I think it's best if I move into the house after this news. Who knows who is out there and what they can do."

"Are you sure Amy can handle that?"

He wanted to tell the attorney she could definitely handle it, but he held his words.

"We'll make it work. We have a good connection, and that puts us halfway there."

"Please check in with me every day. Call me direct.

No need to go through Security Solutions. I'll let them know."

"Will do."

He disconnected the call and restrained himself from throwing the phone across the room. How was it possible no one had thought to dig into the past before this? If he'd known the situation, he'd have already been on top of it. Well, he'd bring his laptop into the house and, while Amy was working on her new game, he'd do his own research. And if he could do it without distressing Amy, he'd see if she knew anything about Harrison Baker's past because it seemed that's where the clue was.

He stripped down to his boxer briefs and began the exercise program the therapist had given him. That's one thing he was religious about. His leg might not ever be 100 percent, but he'd make it the best he could.

When he finished, sweat covered his body and he was shaking from the effort. After filling a glass with water from the fridge, he drank it down in three large gulps, refilled it, and drank again. Then he headed for the shower.

It amused him to see that his cock was still swollen from his adventure with Amy. He'd done his best to keep himself contained, but the damn thing had a mind of its own. He was tempted to take himself in hand to get some relief but nixed that. He wanted it at full throttle tonight when he slid into her bed. He'd just have to call on that famous SEAL control so he didn't overwhelm her and ruin it all.

Finally, he dressed, made sure everything was in his duffel, and carried it all to the house. He wondered if she'd been watching for him because as he headed up the walk between the two buildings, she came to the glass doors and, wonder of wonders, actually slid them open.

But she didn't step outside, he noted. That was okay. They were going to work on it. *After* that fucking asshole Matthew Baker was safely behind bars again. For the time being, he was happy for her to stay inside.

* * *

Matthew was doing his best not to lose it. He had managed to keep himself together for ten years in that hellhole of a prison, once he'd made up his mind what to do. In those years, he'd learned self-discipline, exercised to keep in shape, put up with a hundred tons of shit without striking back, because he had a plan. That plan had kept him focused. But now that his goal was so close, his old companion, impatience, was taking over.

"I think it's a mistake to come back to Tampa so soon," Jamie said as they cruised south on Interstate 75. "I'm still trying to figure out the best way to get you into that house. That's the only place you can get to her because she never leaves it. The place is a fortress, plus there are the security guards."

"The thing to focus on," Matthew said, "is how to breach the security system."

"Working on that. I hacked into the company that installed the system and found a tiny weakness. I've been investigating ways to jam it."

"I thought they were pretty much foolproof by now."

Jamie laughed. "Nothing is 100 percent foolproof. You just have to find its weakness then look on the dark web for ways to exploit it."

Matthew glanced over. "You spend a lot of time on the dark web, do you?"

"Where do you think I got all the information I needed to spring your ass free and do all this other stuff? People have no idea that their weaknesses are out there for others to see if they know how."

"Well, dig a little harder because I want to get this done." The thirst to destroy welled up strong inside him. "She's the last piece of the puzzle, that fucking family that ruined my life."

"Matthew—" Jamie began.

"They did, and don't argue with me. If my father hadn't married that bitch to create the perfect family for himself, doted on their sickening little daughter, and had a new son, none of this would have happened."

"I think you're deluding yourself, but whatever. You know I have my own reasons for doing this."

Matthew laughed. "Which is why this has worked well so far. You have motivation that matches mine."

"And that makes us a perfect team."

"So what about that gizmo you were going to order? When does it arrive?"

"As a matter of fact, I got an email this morning that it will be here today. Remember I told you I rented a virtual post office box? I've had a few things delivered there and, when I get the notification, I can elect to have whatever it is forwarded to wherever I am."

"And it doesn't leave any tracks?"

Jamie smirked. "Using the excellent fake identification I paid for, there's no way anyone can connect it to me. I didn't have to show up in person to do it, either."

"Excellent."

"So I had it forwarded to a parcel pickup place in Tampa. I'll check on it as soon as we hit town. That's the last piece of the puzzle to put our plan into place. But, Matthew?"

"Yeah?" Now what, Matthew thought.

"Please keep it together and just follow the plan. I don't want to see you end up back behind bars."

He snorted. "Me, neither."

Breakfast with Quinn was another pleasant experience. Amy had been so worried that she was reading too much into everything. That last night he'd been taking pity on the poor nutjob. That everything he was doing was nothing more than part of the job he'd been hired for. But the first thing he did when he walked into the house was plant a kiss on her lips.

"Just as delicious as the last time," he told her, heat simmering in his eyes.

She could hardly believe that this hot male actually wanted *her,* when she was sure he could have any woman he wanted. But there was nothing fake about the kiss or the look her gave her.

True to his word, he stashed his things in one of the guest rooms but he took the one closest to the master suite.

"You could really move those things right into my room," she told him, hating the tentative sound in her voice.

"Let's see how this works out. I don't want you to feel suffocated."

She'd smiled at that. "Funny because, for the first time in my life, what I feel is anything but that."

His palms cradling her cheeks were warm against her skin.

"Tonight you can tell me exactly what that feeling is. Okay?"

She nodded.

"You go ahead and do your thing," he told her. "I have some work to do on my laptop anyway. We can take a break when it's time for lunch."

She wanted to ask him what kind of work that was

but figured he'd tell her if it was important. She didn't want him to think she was intruding in his life. At least not until she was sure he wanted her to.

It took a supreme effort of will for her to lock away her memories of last night and this morning and the anticipation of what tonight might bring, but she was able to do it and get into the project. The hours passed quickly what with the game taking every bit of her concentration. It was coming along nicely, however. She reached a point where she could take a break and decided to save her work and do just that. She went in search of Quinn and found him in the family room, kicked back in the recliner with his laptop but his face lined with concentration for whatever was on his screen.

"Knock knock."

He looked up and gave her that killer smile.

"Taking a break?"

She nodded. "I believe it's lunchtime."

He glanced at his watch. "Sure is."

"We have a few choices for lunch—"

He held up his hand then saved his work and shut his laptop.

"I fetched the groceries I bought yesterday. The agency told me there was a great kitchen in the cottage, and I like to putter around, but simple things appeal to me. Comfort food."

"And what did you bring to comfort yourself?"

"How about grilled cheese and tomato soup for lunch."

Amy burst out laughing. "That's my regular standby. And perfect."

"But let me fix it," he insisted then winced. "After all, I did bring the ingredients."

"Works for me."

"Good. Come talk to me while I cook."

She admired the economy of movement as he moved around her kitchen. The same way he did everything. She thought she could spend hours looking at his body, but then he might think she was weird. Wait! She *was* weird. She still couldn't figure out why she appealed to him, but she wasn't going to ask questions.

After lunch, he told her he was going to take a walk around outside again.

"Why? There's nothing new to see. The landscape crew doesn't come again for two more days, and I'm pretty sure after all this time and being checked out thoroughly, my neighbors aren't spying on me."

"I agree, but in the Teams, we learned to check things out then do it again, and after we were satisfied everything was okay, do it one more time. It's saved a lot of people from being killed."

"Oh." Killed. She couldn't help the fear that surged through her at that word.

"Not that I think anyone's out there waiting," he

reassured her. "And I promise you, no one will get to you with me around. It's just my nature, so humor me."

"Okay." She forced herself to relax. "If I go back to work, will you be okay for the rest of the afternoon?"

"Of course." Then heat flared in his eyes. "I'll be thinking about tonight. And speaking of that, we'll need a lot of energy so I thought I'd make the steaks I bought."

"You're going to spoil me," she teased.

"Good. I want to." And there was nothing teasing in his tone of voice.

CHAPTER 11

The steak was delicious as were the side dishes Amy fixed to go with them, but Quinn wasn't sure he actually tasted anything. The only thing on his mind was the night ahead of them. When Amy told him she was going to shower, all he could think about was her naked body with water streaming down it. Her thick brown hair, almost a copper brown, hanging down her back like a mermaid. He had detected a faint odor of whatever lotion she used last night, but it was mingled with the scent of the orgasm she'd given herself.

Stop!

He was going to come right in his jeans like a horny teenager if he didn't stop this. Instead, he cleaned up the kitchen, just like he'd told her he would then headed into the en-suite bathroom he was using to take his own shower. He tried to think of nonsexual things so his damn cock would take a rest, but apparently that was impossible. Finally, he turned off the water, took out the clippers so he could trim his beard, splashed on some aftershave, and tied a towel around his waist.

Finally, after taking one last look at himself, grabbed some condoms from his shaving kit and headed across the hall. Amy's door was partially open, but the only light in the room was the bedside lamp, which bathed everything in a warm, mellow glow. He tapped twice on the door.

"Come in." She spoke in a soft tone.

Here goes, he thought, and pushed the door open. And stopped dead in his tracks. He took in every detail of her, memorizing it so he could pull it out any time he wanted to and enjoy it all over again.

She sat in the middle of the king-sized bed, the pillows plumped behind her, wearing nothing but a tentative smile. The sheets were pulled up only to her waist, exposing the round breasts he'd been fantasizing about, and the dark nipples that made his mouth water. The copper-brown curtain of her hair fell softly to her shoulders, framing a face devoid of all makeup except a swipe of lip gloss.

He was sure he'd never seen anything so beautiful, so delectable and mouth-watering.

"Is everything okay?" She sounded as hesitant as she looked.

Quinn blew out a breath. "Damn straight it's okay. Better than okay."

"I see you also dressed formal," she teased.

"Absolutely. This okay?"

She nodded then caught her lower lip between her teeth. "I have to tell you I'm nervous, Quinn. I know you've had a lot of women and I haven't had sex since, well, longer than forever. I'm not sure I'll—"

He held up a hand. "First of all, I think you have a misconception about the number of women I've been with. More than two but less than fifteen is all I'll admit to, and that's starting when I was fifteen."

Was that even sex, he wondered.

"Oh!"

"Second. This is all brand new, whatever this is between us, so nothing in the past counts. We're both new to the game. That work for you?"

She grinned. "As long as one of us knows what goes where."

"Oh, darlin,' I promise you that won't be a problem." He looked down at his body. "Okay, with you if I ditch this towel?"

She giggled again. "I didn't even bother with that."

She flipped the covers back and, at the sight of her naked body, his mouth went dry and he almost forgot to breathe. He could hardly believe this delectable woman actually wanted *him,* but he was going to do his damnedest to make this good for her. And not just for one night, either.

He dropped the condoms on the nightstand, unknotted the towel and tossed it to the side, trying to ignore the way her eyes widened at the sight of him. He slid in next to her, the sheets soft against his skin, and decided kissing was the best place to begin here. But when he turned to his side, slid an arm around her, and bent his head to hers, she thrust her hands into his hair and pressed her mouth to his. Hard. And open.

"I won't break," she told him against his lips. "Don't treat me like I will. I want everything I've been missing. Everything in the dream I told you about last night. All of it."

Okay, then.

He took command of the situation, turning them so she was beneath him and every luscious curve was pressed into him. He fed from her mouth, drank from it, licked every inch inside of it and slid his tongue over hers, coaxing her to do the same. He nibbled at her jawline, licked the slender column of her neck, and bit lightly on her earlobe. She arched into his mouth, and her breasts pressing into his chest made his own nipples harden painfully.

He took his time, pressing a kiss against the pulse throbbing at the hollow of her throat then drawing a line with the tip of his tongue between her wonderful breasts. He'd planned to work up to things slowly, but her dream from last night kept popping into his head in vivid detail.

Giving in, he slid a hand between them and cupped one small but perfect breast, brushing his thumb back and forth over the nipple and feeling it harden to his touch. Lowering his head, he took the nipple into his mouth, closing his teeth over it in a gentle bite that made her cry out in what he sure hoped was pleasure.

He spent a long time on the one breast before shifting to the other one. He wanted to make this as good for her as he could, give her the maximum amount of pleasure. Because when this was all wrapped up, he had no plans to go anywhere. And he wanted her to want him as much as he desired her.

By the time the second nipple popped from his lips, she was moaning and shifting beneath him, lifting to press her sex against his rigid, swollen cock. Sliding down her body, he strung light kisses all over her stomach, tracing the crease between hip and thigh with his tongue. He did it first to one side and then the other. When he finally slid even lower, she was already moaning and pleading for more.

He nudged her legs apart so he could lie between them and peppered kisses on the inside of each thigh before he got to his ultimate goal. She needed no urging to spread her legs to give him better access to her. With the tip of his tongue, he drew a long line between her folds, relishing the heady taste of her juices, so he did it again. And again. And each time she quivered and moaned beneath him.

At last, through teasing both of them, he spread the lips of her sex, much as she'd described to him from her dream, and lunged his mouth inside. Holy shit! Her taste exploded on his tongue, and he couldn't lick fast enough. He took her clit between his teeth and nibbled, tugging on it then biting gently. Amy wrapped her legs around him and lifted herself up to him, and he lost it.

He thrust two fingers inside her then three, driving them in and out hard and fast. Scraping the tips each time against that hot sweet spot.

"Oh god." She cried it out over and over, doing her best to trap his head between her thighs and keep him there.

The more she did that, the more he wanted from her. Every so often he drew back, just flicking his tongue over her hot clit then going back to work with a vengeance. She was unlike any other woman he'd ever been with, and he didn't want this ever to stop.

She was begging and crying now, and he wanted to see her come. With his fingers and his mouth, he drove her the rest of the way to the peak and she exploded, her flavor bursting on his tongue. He swallowed again and again, wanted every drop of her inside him. And when at last the shudders slowed then subsided, he crawled his way back up her body and pulled her tightly against him.

He could feel her racing heart slow then settle back into a regular beat. When she opened her eyes, they had a sexy, satisfied look to them.

"Okay?" he asked.

"More than." She gave him a slow smile. "But don't think you're getting away with only that."

"Oh, we're hardly finished here." He chuckled. "We've just gotten started."

He held her, giving her another moment to settle herself then turned her over and placed a string of kisses down the length of her spine. She hummed beneath his touch, squirming slightly when he got to her gorgeous ass. He was pretty sure no one had ever used their mouth on her quite this way before, and he took great delight in drawing every possible response from her. For a woman who hadn't had sex in ten years, her responses were a welcome surprise.

He covered every inch of her buttocks then traced their lower curve with the tip of his tongue. She was already squirming beneath him, crying out and moaning and crying for more. At last, when he himself couldn't stand it anymore, when he wanted his shaft sliding into the slick heat of her sex, he turned her over and slid a pillow beneath her hips. His hands actually shook as he rolled on a condom. Then he splayed her out the way he wanted, legs bent and spread wide. He pressed the head of his cock at her opening, grabbed her hips, and drove himself inside.

Asshole! Use a little finesse, for fuck's sake.

But when he slid partially out and tried to stop for a moment, she wrapped her legs around his waist, digging her heels into the small of his back, and squeezed him against her.

"I don't want to hurt you," he protested, his voice breathless.

"You'll hurt me if you don't get moving." Her laugh was fractured. "I haven't wanted this for so long, not until you walked through my door. Don't make me beg."

God! He was the one who should be begging.

"You got it, darlin'."

His every intention had been to take it slow and easy with her, draw it out, but she was like a tiger unleashed, and his own hunger was at its peak. Holding her hips, he began a steady in and out glide, slow at first then faster and faster. She was there with him every inch of the way, even stroking her own clit as she'd done in her dream.

The explosion when it came was cataclysmic. It shook them both, consuming every bit of them as spasm after spasm roared through them. He had no idea how long it lasted, how long they rocked together, shuddering, letting the orgasm wring every last bit of response from them.

At last the spasms slowed and then subsided. Amy eased her legs from around his waist, and he leaned down to wrap his arms around her. He sprinkled kisses on her face before holding her cheeks in his hands and kissing her lips. He was almost afraid to look in her eyes, to see what was there. Was she disappointed? Upset? Ready to go back into her shell? If she did, he'd just work twice as hard to break her out again, but he hoped…

"Don't look so apprehensive," she teased in her soft voice. "It was better than my dream, a hundred times."

She brushed his hair back from his damp forehead. "Can we do it again?"

He burst out laughing. "As many times as you want. But first, let me get rid of this condom and rest a little. I'm not as young as I used to be."

"Quinn?" She held his head and forced him to look at her before he moved.

"Hmmm?"

"You aren't just a body. I want you to know that. If it's not you, it won't be anyone."

"Are you sure? It's been…"

"A ten-year disaster for me. But I think I was waiting for you all this time."

"Me, too." He eased from her body. "You just hold those thoughts. I'll be right back."

As he headed to the bathroom, all he could think was he was one lucky bastard. And no one, not a single person, was going to hurt her. They'd have to go through him, and that wasn't happening.

Amy was lying there with nothing covering her when he climbed back into bed. He rolled her against him and tugged up the sheet.

"How about a little nap before we do this again? I warn you, I might want to do it all night."

She grinned. "Works for me."

CHAPTER 12

"I believe we are all set."

Jamie stood at the dining room table of the suite they were renting in the quaint but luxurious hotel about twenty-five miles outside of Tampa. Matthew looked at everything assembled there.

"Tell me again about the RF jammer you bought. You're the electronics expert. Are you sure this one will work?"

Jamie nodded. "From as far as fifty feet away. We can park the car two streets away, stroll over there about an hour after dark, and disable her fancy home security system. This is the best money can buy, and I studied them all. We'll be able to climb over the fence and get to the house. I hacked the security system, so if it goes silent it won't send an alarm for an hour."

"And how do we get inside again?"

"There's a big sliding glass door at the back of the

house, the side that faces the little guest cottage. I've got a glass cutter that will get us inside, but we need to wait until after dark."

"Fine. Fine." Matthew jumped up and began to pace. "Does she stay up late at night? Watch television? What? We need to know which room she'll be in."

"I have not been able to get exact information," Jamie protested, "because I couldn't get into the house. And no one I'm paying off is there at night. You know that."

"Right, right, right. I hate having to wing it, but I guess we have no choice." He jingled the change in his pocket as he paced. "Fuck, Jamie. I want to get it done."

"I know." Jamie's voice was soothing. "But we have to do it right. All those years of planning, all my hard work, all the bribe money we've paid out. Let's not blow it by moving too fast or at the wrong time."

"I know." Matthew sighed and dropped into the chair again. "But we're a definite go for tomorrow night, right?"

Jamie nodded. "One reason is because a thunderstorm is predicted. Electricity can be uncertain. Neighbors won't be out walking their dogs. All the elements will be in our favor."

"We're leaving here at nine o'clock."

"Yes, Matt. Nine o'clock. With one thing and another, that will get us to her house at ten. I'm pretty sure she'll be in bed by then, if not asleep. Nothing I've found shows her to be a night owl."

Matthew grinned. "Good. Let's get some dinner."

* * *

Amy indulged in a long, leisurely stretch before she opened her eyes, relishing the feel of a sated, well-loved, *well-fucked* body. Last night had been many things, the biggest being a miracle. Ten years ago, she had never expected to ever be with a man again. Ever enjoy sex. Never have anything to look forward to. She saw her days as an endless stretch locked to her computer and hidden away from the outside world.

Quinn Molloy had changed all that. That a man like him could have feelings for her was the biggest miracle of all.

"Penny for them."

The deep, husky voice made her turn her head. Quinn was lying stretched out next to her, on his side, his head braced on his hand, his mouth turned up in a grin.

Her laugh was soft. "Oh, they're worth a lot more. But I think I'd need a lot more of last night to be able to explain them."

Now it was his turn to laugh.

"Lord. I didn't know I had an insatiable woman on my hands."

She touched her hand to his cheek. "Only for you. Quinn, you are the greatest miracle in my life. I don't know how or why you feel this way about it, but I'm praying you don't change your mind."

"No worries there. I have no interest in anyone or anyplace else."

She pushed up in bed, ignoring the fact that the covers left her naked from the waist up. "But, is this a temporary assignment for you? Or are you just going to be paid to be my live-in bodyguard forever? What if something else comes along?"

"Not gonna happen. And I don't know what the future holds for me, except you will definitely be in it. The first project is to help you step out into the world again, and that's going to take some time. And even when we reach that point, I'm still not leaving. If you're okay by yourself, I can work local jobs for Security Solutions."

"You really want to do that?" She held her breath.

He cradled her head in his hands. "I really want to do that. I'll keep telling you as many times as I have to until you believe it."

"Good." She grinned. "Then I think you deserve a big breakfast for that."

"Certainly after last night," he teased. "You wore me out, lady."

"Look who's talking!" She threw back the covers and stood up. "I'm for a quick shower and breakfast. How about you?"

"I'd say let's shower together and save water, except then we'd get nothing done all day. I need to do my exercises for my leg, and you have work to do this morning. So, meet you in the kitchen?"

"You bet. Now, get out of here so I can get things done."

She hummed to herself all through the shower, and while she threw on yoga pants and a T-shirt. And while she assembled all the ingredients for the meal. She even opened the sliding door and stood in the opening with her orange juice, thinking maybe today was the day to take those first steps outside. Her good mood lasted until Quinn came into the kitchen with a tight look on his face.

"What is it?" she asked. "What's wrong?"

"Dan Rendell called."

Her heart dropped to her feet. Dan wouldn't be calling again so soon unless there was a problem.

Quinn took her hands and led her over to the kitchen table. "Sit down, Amy. Let me get you some coffee."

She didn't want to sit, but she didn't argue. She wanted answers.

Quinn set a mug of her favorite coffee in front of her and took the chair cornerwise to hers so he could face her.

"I apologize for this, but we've been holding something back from you. I thought you should know, but Rendell hoped it would be resolved before we had to say anything."

"Know what, Quinn? It's about Matthew, right?"

He nodded. "I don't know any other way to say this except straight out. Matthew Baker escaped from prison last week."

"Last week?" She stared at him. "How? I mean, what happened? And why did Dan decide to keep it from me?"

"I think you know the answer to that, sweetheart. Your fear of him has kept you a prisoner for ten years. Even though he supposedly thought you were dead. And everyone hoped he'd be caught before we had to tell you."

"So your coming here was all a big setup." She felt sick at how easily she believed in him.

"No. Get that out of your head. Security Solutions had already offered me a job before I even 'met' you. And I would have come here even without it. But I wanted to be with you in person, Amy, and this seemed ideal. Rendell was insisting you have on-site security, I was available and qualified, and it gave me a chance to connect with you in person." He took her hands and wrapped his big ones around them. "I think I fell in love with you that first night online. Even if no one was paying me, I'd be here, and I'm staying, so get anything else out of your head. Okay?"

She swallowed then nodded her head. She wanted so badly to believe him.

"Why did Dan call you just now? What's been happening? What came up?"

He told her about the US Marshal service nationwide manhunt. About scoping out all the places where he might go to hide and the fact there was no trace of him anywhere.

"Wait." She took a sip of the hot coffee. "As far as he's concerned, I'm dead, so why would I be in any danger?"

So then he told her about her grave being dug up and the coffin pried open.

"Oh my god!" She began to shake so hard Quinn took the mug from her hands and set it on the table.

He wrapped his hands around her shaking ones and squeezed.

"There's more."

For a moment, she thought she might pass out. "More? What kind of more?"

"When no one could find any trace of him, they suggested looking into your stepfather's background. Did you know anything about him before he married your mother, except that he had a crazy son who was a big problem in your family?"

She shook her head, afraid of what he was going to say next.

"I suggested to Harrison that he look even further back, to any details surrounding Harrison's first wife."

"And?"

"It turns out that wife brought an illegitimate child to the marriage, an odd situation for a big corporate attorney. Although, apparently she came from a well-respected family, and she'd forced them to acknowledge her child. They were damn happy when Harrison married her."

"I bet. So, what about the child?"

"A girl. Named Jamie. Two years old at the time, which makes her four years older than Matthew. *Now* we learn they had an unhealthy relationship. That every time Matthew walked out, he ran to Jamie. That the last couple of years before that awful night, they were in the drug business. Harrison had settled a large amount of money on him—"

She waved her hand. "We knew about that."

He went on to tell her about the growing bank account Jamie also had access to. About the guard they bribed to carry messages back and forth so there'd be nothing linking her to him. And on and on and on.

Quinn nodded. "Someone just as odd as he was. Now Rendell thinks every time Matthew disappeared from your home, he was with her."

"They're friends," she guessed.

"And maybe more, but let's not get into that right now."

Amy forced herself to take a deep breath and sit still, when she really wanted to jump back in bed and pull the covers over her head. She tried to absorb it all while Quinn filled her in on all the other underhanded things they'd done to learn she was alive and find out where she was.

"But the thing is, when they learned all that, that Matthew had help, they focused the search on Tampa because they knew you were his target. The Marshals put a full team on it and circulated their pictures to all the law enforcement agencies in the area. And they've both been spotted here." He gave a humorless laugh. "They only spotted him because he was with her. He changed his appearance some, but she didn't bother, probably figuring no one would be after her. Until this week, she was right."

Now Amy really thought she was going to pass out.

"We have to get out of here, Quinn. Have to find a place to hide. Someplace. Anyplace. Now."

She started to rise, but he stopped her.

"No, we're not. You're done running. The storm tonight is a perfect cover for them, and the Hillsborough County Sheriff's office spotted them getting coffee at a Starbucks. By accident, as a matter of fact, but a lucky break for us."

"So, what happens now?"

He took both her hands in his. "The Marshals have a team on their way here, plus Security Solutions is sending two agents to help. And a car will be patrolling the neighborhood."

"Won't he see them?"

Quinn shook his head. "The sheriff's deputies who spotted them are in an unmarked car, as it happens, and are broadcasting their progress to the Marshals. It's all good."

"But—"

"But the important thing is, I'm going to make sure

you're safe. Trust me on that. We're making arrangements because all indications are that he's getting ready to make his move. But, I promise, he'll never get to you."

Even after a half hour, she wasn't convinced, but she decided to follow Quinn's directions. It began to rain later that morning which helped. Four Marshals arrived in civilian clothing, pretending there was electrical damage from the storm and checking the outside. The fifth was dressed as a housekeeper to fool anyone watching the house. When the woman tugged off her disguise, she was dressed in jeans and a shirt with a badge pinned to the pocket and her gun in a holster at her waist.

She was Amy's size and immediately requisitioned some of her clothes.

"Just in case," she told Amy. "If he gets in and grabs anyone, it will be me, and he will not be happy with the outcome."

"You *want* them to break in," she told the Marshal.

"We do. That way we can catch him in the act and get him out of your life for good. This time in a high security prison."

"See?" Quinn told her. "It will all work out."

"But what if they don't try their stuff tonight?" Amy asked. "We can't go through this every night. They'll know we're onto them."

"Then we'll look at other options. But Jamie picked up some kind of order at a package mailbox place today and everything else they've done indicates they'll take advantage of the storm to get in here."

"What about the security system?"

"There's a possibility it's an RF signal jammer to jam your security system," one of the Marshals told her. "Like those thieves who were robbing houses in your neighborhood had. That's okay. We're going to let their little act play out. We're ready for them."

Amy thought she'd go out of her mind during the day. The vans were hidden on the far side of the garage, and everyone kept out of sight. If not for Quinn, Amy was sure she'd have lost her mind. But he never left her side, his gun strapped to his thigh. He fed her tea and toast and soup. Rubbed her back and shoulders. And never let her out of his sight. The Marshals made themselves invisible, the van that brought the housekeeper earlier showed up again and left as if carrying its passenger. As the weather grew worse, Quinn closed all the shutters on the windows so no one could see in. Also, the blinds on the sliding doors.

By nine o'clock, the storm was going full blast, thunder booming and lightning crackling in the sky. Amy huddled in her bedroom with Quinn, while two of the Marshals went through the usual nightly routine for her and Quinn.

Minus the sex, of course!

Quinn fed her tea and massaged her back again and whispered soothing words to her. Then, just after nine, there came a boom of thunder louder than any of the others, and the power went out.

"The security system has a backup," she reminded Quinn.

"It takes a few minutes to kick in, remember? Just sit tight with me."

They had moved the laptop monitor into her room and plugged it into a battery pack so they could watch what was going on. The moment the pictures disappeared, Quinn yelled out to the Marshals.

"They're here," the man who hurried into their room told them. The power isn't out anywhere but in your house. They've jammed your security and killed your power. Quinn, you keep your gun ready and don't leave her side."

"No worries there."

Waiting was hard, but before long they heard the sliding door in the family room open. It had a slight squeak that distinguished it.

Then Matthew spoke. "Got you now, you little bitch. Get your ass over here before I slit your boyfriend open."

Next they heard, "US Marshals. Drop the gun and knife."

Two shots were fired, and screams split the air, underscored with guttural cursing.

"You can come out," one of the Marshals called.

"Let's go, darlin'."

Quinn took her hand and led her into the family

room. She nearly fainted at what she saw. A tall, thin woman Amy guessed was in her early thirties had her hands cuffed behind her. Blood streaked down one arm from a long cut. Matthew sat on the floor, arms cuffed behind him, blood oozing from a shoulder wound. The look he gave her made everything inside her freeze.

"There you are, you prissy little bitch." He looked at Quinn. "You know the name she's using isn't real, right? Her real name is Hallie Baker. My *father's* name. My asshole father who gave up on us when he married her bitch of a mother and sent her off to live with a prune-faced aunt. But I found her." His laugh was anything but humorous. "We're alike, Jamie and I. We belong together."

The look he gave Amy would have shriveled another person, but she just moved closer to Quinn, who pulled her close to his side.

"You know she's a nutjob, right?" Matthew looked at Quinn when he said it.

"Actually," Quinn said, "I think you're the crazy one."

"That's right." One of the Marshals nodded in agreement. "Every effort is going to be made to get you locked up in one of those supermax prisons where you'll never see the light of day."

"Bitch!" Jamie screamed. "If not for you, my stepfather wouldn't have thrown us out, but he just wanted his perfect little doll and his perfect little boy. We were just trash to him." She laughed, an insane sound. "Well, he's dead now. All of them are." Then she looked at Matthew. "Don't worry, sugar. We've got plenty of money. I'll get us the best damn lawyers, and before long we'll be off on one of those islands fucking like bunnies."

Amy thought she was going to be sick. So this was the person who had been helping Matthew all this time. There was an unhealthy vibe between them, underscored by the woman's words, and Amy had no desire to know the details of their relationship. But at least they all knew who had made things happen.

Amy dug deep for some courage and stared at her stepbrother. "You won't be off on any island with anyone. You'll be alive, buried away in a supermax prison, and Jamie will be locked away in another, both of you knowing every single day that I'm free and you're not."

Jamie and Matthew began screaming again. By now more Marshals had arrived with two vans, one to transport each passenger. Amy watched as their ankles were cuffed and hobbled and each was dragged out by two Marshals.

"Hey," Jamie yelled. "We're wounded. We need medical attention. What if we bleed out?"

"Save the state a ton of money," one of the Marshals told her as they hauled her out the door.

Finally, after shaking hands with Quinn and Amy and leaving their cards, they were gone.

Quinn pulled out his phone and called Dan Rendell,

giving him a report, nodding as he listened to the other man. Conversation over, he turned to Amy.

"I'd say you might be happier if we slept somewhere else tonight, but I know that's still a bridge we have to cross. You okay?"

"I'm still in shock," she told him, "but I have to say it wasn't as bad as I expected. He didn't get his hands on me, and when I looked at him, I realized he's just a pathetic lunatic. He's the one who will suffer where he's going." She leaned into him. "But I don't think I'd have made it through this without you."

"Good." He kissed her forehead. "Keep thinking that. Like I told you. I'm not going anywhere. Ever."

EPILOGUE

"That's it. Two more steps. Just like we've done each day. Come on, sweetheart. You can do it."

She was on the patio a couple of feet outside the open sliding doors, a distance that still seemed enormous to her. Quinn stood about a foot away from her, his hand reaching out for her as it had for so many days now, an encouraging smile on his face.

A month had passed since that horrendous night. The US Marshals had reported that both Matthew and Jamie were locked away. She had yet to stand trial, but Matthew was now in a supermax prison and no one would ever hear from him again.

Quinn had insisted she take a week and do nothing but hang out with him. No coding video games. No online research. Nothing but being pampered—by him—and learning the pleasure of sex with him all over again.

Two weeks ago, he had started coaxing her outside. There was no bogeyman out there anymore. Whatever else had frightened her had disappeared with Matthew and Jamie.

"I wonder if I sensed her out there," she said to Quinn one night, "and that was a factor in my never leaving the house."

"Well, if it was, she's gone, and it's time to get on with our lives."

In the beginning, all she could do was stand in the open doorway while Quinn sat on the patio talking to her. Then she finally took one step out, and another, and another. The day she took four steps out they had a major celebration. He made dinner for her, and she spent the night in a cloud of the best sex she'd ever had.

Since then, they'd been working on adding a step each day.

Today was her birthday. Dan Rendell had flown out to celebrate it with her, as well as Tex and Melody who were staying in the cottage. They all stood on the patio, around the table where her birthday cake held the place of honor. All she had to do was walk to it.

"That's it, darlin'." Quinn held her hand, leading her one step at a time.

She started to shake but forced herself to keep moving. She could do this. She had a good life now. A man who loved her and who was now working for Security Solutions on local assignments. Her own video games corporation that Dan had set up for her.

And two wonderful friends in Tex and Melody. She was outside, and the world hadn't fallen in on her.

"One more step," Quinn coaxed. "There you go."

She blew out a shaky breath when she reached the table. Quinn pulled her into a big hug then kissed her so intensely Melody and Tex whistled.

"Cake time," Dan told her. "And champagne."

He filled everyone's glass while Melody cut the cake. Then Quinn lifted his glass in a toast.

"Here's to the best thing that ever happened to me. The woman I've fallen in love with, and who I hope will marry me as soon as I can convince her to say yes."

The others whistled and cheered, raised their glasses, and drank from them.

Amy cleared her throat. "And to Tex and Melody, without whom I'd never have met Quinn and changed my life." She looked at Quinn. "And the answer's yes. Absolutely."

"Time to make wedding plans," Melody told her. "And trust me, that's the best decision you'll ever make."

"Don't I know it," she agreed, and lifted her face for Quinn's kiss.

Nightmares were gone, and there was just the good life ahead.

ABOUT THE AUTHOR

I love to hear from my readers. You can write to me at *authordesireeholt@gmail.com* I hope you will do that.

Where else can you find me?

First and foremost, I hope you will join my reader group. It's a fun place to be.

www.desiremeonly.com

www.desireeholt.com

Facebook: www.facebook.com/authordesireeholt

Twitter: @desireeholt

Pinterest: www.pinterest.com/desiree02holt

facebook.com/authordesireeholt
twitter.com/desireeholt
pinterest.com/desiree02holt

ALSO BY DESIREE HOLT

I hope you enjoyed Amy and Quinn's story. Writing it was a true labor of love for me. And I also hope you will check out my other stories in Susan Stoker's Special Forces World.

Protecting Maddie

When Maddie Winslow talked a student out of his gun in her classroom, she never figured it would set off a chain of events that put her life in grave danger, and the lives of her parents.

Hiding in WitSec for thirty years, her parents thought they had beaten the odds—until the image of Maddie, an identical replica of her mother—hits the television airwaves and the people who have been seeking revenge all these years find her. Intent on learning where her mother is hiding, they break into her home and then try to kidnap her. Frightened, she goes to her friend, Zee, who once dated someone in Delta Force. She calls him to explain her friend's situation, but he's prepping for a mission and can't leave the base.

Hunter "Hawkeye" St. John, a Delta Force team member, is on medical leave recuperating in Tampa and chafing for some action. When the he and Maddie meet, the sparks flying between them sizzle the air. But if Hawkeye wants to move forward with Maddie he first has to keep her safe and then eliminate the bad guys.

Protecting Cassie

Injured and discharged, he is lost...

Sam Alvarez is newly discharged from SEALs that had been his entire life. Without the Team he is lost, but a bad injury to his left arm ended his career. His rehab is slow and he resents everything. The tiny isolated cabin in Maine former SEAL John "Tex" Keenan found for him is just what he wants.

Frightened and in hiding...

Physical therapist Cassie Malone had a job she loved, great friends and a man in her life she thought was Prince Charming. Until by accident she discovered he's one of Boston's drug kingpins. Now she's hiding out in tiny Castile and scared he'll find her.

Heat and danger collide...

When Fate throws Cassie and Sam together, it's a battle for him to let her help him relearn everything. His surliness is in high gear and she's always looking over her shoulder. But neither of them counted on or expected the hot, hot attraction blazing between them. When drug smugglers show up and put everyone in danger, including Cassie, it's up to Sam to use his skills to take them down and save the woman he's come to love. But can he do it before it's too late?

There are many more books in this fan fiction world than listed here, for an up-to-date list go to www.AcesPress.com

You can also visit our Amazon page at: http://www.amazon.com/author/operationalpha

Special Forces: Operation Alpha World

Denise Agnew: Dangerous to Hold
Shauna Allen: Awakening Aubrey
Shauna Allen: Defending Danielle
Shauna Allen: Rescuing Rebekah
Shauna Allen: Saving Scarlett
Shauna Allen: Saving Grace
Brynne Asher: Blackburn
Jennifer Becker: Hiding Catherine
Julia Bright: Saving Lorelei
Julia Bright: Rescuing Amy
Victoria Bright: Surviving Savage
Victoria Bright: Going Ghost
Victoria Bright: Jostling Joker
Cara Carnes: Protecting Mari
Kendra Mei Chailyn: Beast
Kendra Mei Chailyn: Barbie
Kendra Mei Chailyn : Pitbull
Melissa Kay Clarke: Rescuing Annabeth
Melissa Kay Clarke: Safeguarding Miley
Samantha A. Cole: Handling Haven
Samantha A. Cole: Cheating the Devil

Sue Coletta: Hacked
Melissa Combs: Gallant
KaLyn Cooper: Rescuing Melina
Liz Crowe: Marking Mariah
Jordan Dane: Redemption for Avery
Jordan Dane: Fiona's Salvation
Riley Edwards: Protecting Olivia
Riley Edwards: Redeeming Violet
Riley Edwards, Recovering Ivy
Nicole Flockton: Protecting Maria
Nicole Flockton: Guarding Erin
Nicole Flockton: Guarding Suzie
Nicole Flockton: Guarding Brielle
Casey Hagen: Shielding Nebraska
Casey Hagen: Shielding Harlow
Casey Hagen: Shielding Josie
Casey Hagen: Shielding Blair
Desiree Holt: Protecting Maddie
Kathy Ivan: Saving Sarah
Kathy Ivan: Saving Savannah
Kathy Ivan: Saving Stephanie
Jesse Jacobson: Protecting Honor
Jesse Jacobson: Fighting for Honor
Jesse Jacobson: Defending Honor
Jesse Jacobson: Summer Breeze
Silver James: Rescue Moon
Silver James: SEAL Moon
Silver James: Assassin's Moon
Silver James: Under the Assassin's Moon

Becca Jameson: Saving Sofia
Kate Kinsley: Protecting Ava
Heather Long: Securing Arizona
Heather Long: Guarding Gertrude
Heather Long: Protecting Pilar
Heather Long: Covering Coco
Gennita Low: No Protection
Kirsten Lynn: Joining Forces for Jesse
Margaret Madigan: Bang for the Buck
Margaret Madigan: Buck the System
Margaret Madigan: Jungle Buck
Margaret Madigan: December Chill
Rachel McNeely: The SEAL's Surprise Baby
Rachel McNeely: The SEAL's Surprise Bride
Rachel McNeely: The SEAL's Surprise Twin
KD Michaels: Saving Laura
KD Michaels: Protecting Shane
KD Michaels: Avenging Angels
Wren Michaels: The Fox & The Hound
Wren Michaels: The Fox & The Hound 2
Wren Michaels: Shadow of Doubt
Wren Michaels: Shift of Fate
Wren Michaels: Steeling His Heart
Kat Mizera: Protecting Bobbi
Mary B Moore: Force Protection
LeTeisha Newton: Protecting Butterfly
LeTeisha Newton: Protecting Goddess
LeTeisha Newton: Protecting Vixen
LeTeisha Newton: Protecting Heartbeat

MJ Nightingale: Protecting Beauty
MJ Nightingale: Betting on Benny
MJ Nightingale: Protecting Secrets
Sarah O'Rourke: Saving Liberty
Debra Parmley: Protecting Pippa
Debra Parmley: Split Screen Scream
Lainey Reese: Protecting New York
Jenika Snow: Protecting Lily
Jen Talty: Burning Desire
Jen Talty: Burning Kiss
Jen Talty: Burning Skies
Jen Talty: Burning Lies
Jen Talty: Burning Heart
Megan Vernon: Protecting Us
Megan Vernon: Protecting Earth

Police and Fire: Operation Alpha World

Freya Barker: Burning for Autumn
KaLyn Cooper: Justice for Gwen
Aspen Drake: Sheltering Emma
Deanndra Hall: Shelter for Sharla
Deanndra Hall:Justice for Aleta
Barb Han: Kace
Reina Torres: Justice for Sloane
Stacey Wilk: Stage Fright

As you know, this book included at least one character from Susan Stoker's books. To check out more, see below.

SEAL of Protection: Legacy Series

Securing Caite
Securing Brenae (novella)
Securing Sidney
Securing Piper
Securing Zoey (Jan 2020)
Securing Avery (May 2020)
Securing Kalee (Sept 2020)

Delta Team Two Series

Shielding Gillian (Apr 2020)
Shielding Kinley (Aug 2020)
Shielding Aspen (Oct 2020)
Shielding Riley (TBA)
Shielding Devyn (TBA)
Shielding Ember (TBA)
Shielding Sierra (TBA)

Delta Force Heroes Series

Rescuing Rayne (FREE!)
Rescuing Aimee (novella)
Rescuing Emily
Rescuing Harley
Marrying Emily (novella)
Rescuing Kassie

Rescuing Bryn
Rescuing Casey
Rescuing Sadie (novella)
Rescuing Wendy
Rescuing Mary
Rescuing Macie (Novella)

Badge of Honor: Texas Heroes Series

Justice for Mackenzie (FREE!)
Justice for Mickie
Justice for Corrie
Justice for Laine (novella)
Shelter for Elizabeth
Justice for Boone
Shelter for Adeline
Shelter for Sophie
Justice for Erin
Justice for Milena
Shelter for Blythe
Justice for Hope
Shelter for Quinn
Shelter for Koren
Shelter for Penelope

SEAL of Protection Series

Protecting Caroline (FREE!)
Protecting Alabama
Protecting Fiona
Marrying Caroline (novella)

Protecting Summer
Protecting Cheyenne
Protecting Jessyka
Protecting Julie (novella)
Protecting Melody
Protecting the Future
Protecting Kiera (novella)
Protecting Alabama's Kids (novella)
Protecting Dakota

New York Times, USA Today and *Wall Street Journal* Bestselling Author Susan Stoker has a heart as big as the state of Tennessee where she lives, but this all American girl has also spent the last fourteen years living in Missouri, California, Colorado, Indiana, and Texas. She's married to a retired Army man who now gets to follow *her* around the country.

www.stokeraces.com
www.AcesPress.com
susan@stokeraces.com

Made in the USA
Lexington, KY
21 November 2019